SAVOR YOU

SAVOR YOU

A Fusion Novel

Kristen Proby

WM

WILLIAM MORROW
An Imprint of HarperCollinsPublishers

SAVOR YOU. Copyright © 2018 by Kristen Proby. All rights reserved. Printed in the United States of America. No part of this book may be used or reproduced in any manner whatsoever without written permission except in the case of brief quotations embodied in critical articles and reviews. For information, address HarperCollins Publishers, 195 Broadway, New York, NY 10007.

HarperCollins books may be purchased for educational, business, or sales promotional use. For information, please email the Special Markets Department at SPsales@harpercollins.com.

FIRST EDITION

Designed by Diahann Sturge

Library of Congress Cataloging-in-Publication Data has been applied for.

ISBN 978-0-06-267489-0

18 19 20 21 22 LSC 10 9 8 7 6 5 4 3 2 1

This book is for Sarah.
Thank you for all the beautiful menus in these books,
and for being a wonderful human. xo

Prologue

~Mia~

"Are you kidding me?" I stare at my doctor, dumbfounded. *Are you motherfucking kidding me?*

"I'm not," she says with a satisfied grin and pats my knee. "False-positive pregnancy tests are more common than you think."

"But the whole damn purpose of a pregnancy test is to tell the *truth*."

My fingers are shaking now. Oh my God, what did I *do*?

"Well, it can't think for itself. And sometimes it's wrong."

"Sometimes it's wrong." I swallow hard so I don't throw up all over her. "He married me," I whisper. "We've only been married for *four days*."

"You can always keep trying to have children," she says.

"You don't understand. He married me because the pregnancy test was positive." I swallow again and impatiently brush at the tears on my cheeks.

"Mia, that's no way to keep a man—"

"No." I shake my head and glare at her. "I didn't do it on purpose. I just got pregnant, and the next thing I knew we were at the justice of the peace."

"I was twenty once," she says and pats my knee again, and I want to deck her condescending ass. "Young people can be impulsive. I'm sure you can have the marriage annulled if that's what you want to do. In the meantime, I recommend you going on the pill."

The rest of the appointment is a blur of prescriptions and another pat on the knee, and then I'm in my car, staring at the plain gold band on my left hand, sobbing.

There's no other reason for Camden to be married to me. He's never told me he loves me. Hell, we never even officially said we were dating. We moved in together as roommates, and it evolved into hot and convenient sex.

He was just doing the right thing.

And now I have to do the right thing, too.

I can fix this.

No one knows that we got married. Not even my best friends.

And he won't be home for at least another four hours from his shift at the pub.

Once I'm in our small Seattle apartment, I start blindly throwing my things into suitcases, and when those run out I use garbage bags.

I have to go before he gets home. I can't face him. I can't

tell him that I was stupid and maybe too hopeful that a sexy and driven man could truly want to be with me.

Once my car is loaded, I write a short note.

Camden,

My doctor assured me today that the pregnancy test was wrong. I'm not pregnant. There was no need to be hasty and get married. We are free to find someone we truly love to spend our lives with.

Best wishes,
Mia

I lay the paper on the kitchen counter and take one last look around our apartment. We've only lived here for three months, but there are so many memories. Sex, and food, and laughter.

But there wasn't any love, at least not from Camden.

And in spite of all of my faults, I deserve love, too.

Chapter One

~Mia~

*O*h, hello Camden." I smile and tilt my head ever-so-slightly to the side. I'm standing in our office in front of the large full-length mirror between mine and Addie's desks. "Thank you. I've let it grow since I last saw you. No time to get a haircut when you run a successful restaurant."

I sigh and stare at myself in the mirror. "Don't brag. That's not nonchalant." I narrow my freshly lined eyes and consider what to say. "What's that? You've missed me? How nice. I admit that I've hardly given you a thought in the past ten years."

I smirk and then roll my eyes. That's the biggest lie of my life.

"No, I've never watched your show." I practice raising just one eyebrow, not quite as menacing as The Rock, but in that sophisticated way that some women can do, like my best friend Addie, and fail miserably. Both eyebrows go up and I just look surprised.

"So, you're impotent." I nod sagely and try to look sympathetic. "That must be horrible for you."

"Who the fuck are you talking to?" Riley, another of my best friends and co-owner of Seduction, asks as she hurries into our office.

"No one," I reply with a sigh and tease my hair for the fortieth time. "I'm practicing what to say when I see Camden."

"I don't think you should lead with a conversation about his dick," she says and then chuckles. "Although, it's the most unique icebreaker I've ever heard of, so do whatever works for you."

"It's been ten years," I whisper. "How is this even happening?"

"Why didn't you tell us about him?" Riley counters and I turn to face her.

"Because he was a dude I dated in culinary school. It wasn't serious."

"You freaking *married* him."

I shrug and turn away, still avoiding the conversation. "Well, I'm not married to him now, am I? And it's just my luck that he became a celebrity chef and that he's going to be in *my* kitchen. Does God hate me?"

"I've seen Camden," Riley says with a slow smile. "He's a sexy celebrity chef. Eye candy in your kitchen isn't a horrible thing."

I shake my head. If it were anyone but Camden I would agree. But the man got *hotter* in the last ten years.

How does that even happen?

"You know how I feel about sharing my kitchen."

"You've made it quite clear," she says with a laugh. "It's not forever. By the time we're ready to tape episodes for the show, we'll be on a set. For now, Trevor wants you guys to meet and to start brainstorming recipe ideas and get to know each other a bit."

"If we're in competition with each other, why do we need to get to know each other? I should be able to just show up and kick his ass and then call it a day."

She smirks. "There's nothing spontaneous about spontaneous television."

I frown and cross my arms over my chest, but Riley immediately wraps her arms around me and gives me a tight hug. I don't love to be touched, so I stiffen, but that just makes her hold on harder.

"You're touching me."

"I love you, Mia."

Damn it. "I love you, too."

"You're not a grouchy woman," she says and I can't help but grin. "You're beautiful and you're a genius in the kitchen."

"Now you're just sucking up."

She kisses my cheek and pulls away. I rub the spot on my cheek and sigh. "Fine. I'll turn the grouchy level down a bit. You know, all I ever wanted was to cook. I just wanted to open this place with you guys and cook delicious food. I never signed on to be a TV chef."

"I know," she says with a nod. "And you've been—"

"Difficult."

"Awesome about it."

I try to cock my brow again, but it doesn't work.

"You may grumble, but you still do what we ask, and that's more than I ever expected. I don't know how you feel about meeting with Camden today because you don't ever *talk* to us about it, but I can tell you this. You're beautiful. That blue top looks amazing. He's going to swallow his tongue."

"I don't care," I lie.

"Honey, you're a woman. Of course you care." She checks the time on her phone. "He should be here any minute. We're meeting in the bar."

"Not the kitchen?"

"No, you can show him your kitchen yourself. It's your space."

She turns to leave, and I take one last look in the mirror. "You've got this. He's just a man, and you've got this."

I nod confidently, smooth my hands down my black skirt, and flip my curly black hair behind my shoulder as I leave the safety of my office and walk to the bar.

Our restaurant is simply stunning. If I didn't own it, I would *love* to work here. We've expanded recently, adding two dozen more tables. The grey hardwood floors gleam in the low light. The chairs are plush and inviting, and the booths are deep, framed by heavy curtains for a more intimate experience. Not to mention, the food is remarkable if I do say so myself.

I walk into the bar and immediately spot Camden. His

back is to me, but I'd recognize him anywhere. He's a bit broader now, his shoulders and arms nicely wrapped in his white button-down shirt. But his hair is the same light brown, if a bit longer than before. It used to beg for my fingers to mess it up. And let's be honest, even sitting down, I'd recognize his ass anywhere.

He's talking with Trevor, the show's executive producer and Riley's new husband. Riley is there, along with Addie, Cami, and Kat—the other co-owners of Seduction, and my very best friends.

I take a deep breath and wrap all of the confidence I can muster around me, then walk steadily to the table.

"Hello."

Camden turns with a smile, and I swear everything in me just *stills*. I can't smile, or walk, or even give him the up and down once-over greeting that I'd decided upon last night. All I can do is stare into his deep-blue eyes, and lock my knees so I don't fall on my ass.

Damn him.

"Mia." Hearing my name from his lips feels like an out-of-body experience. "How are you?"

"I'm well," I reply and hold my hand out for his. He shakes it, but rather than let go, he kisses the back of my hand. The girls give each other looks of surprise and I quickly retrieve my own hand. "And you?"

"I'm great."

Someone, Kat I think, puts a glass of wine in my hand and I take a long sip, needing the liquid courage.

"You know each other?" Trevor asks, but he already knows the answer to that. I'm sure Riley told him everything she knows, which isn't much.

"We used to," Camden says, still holding my gaze. "A long time ago."

"A long time," I agree with a nod and walk to the opposite side of the table. I can't sit next to him without smelling him, and the fact that he still smells the same doesn't bode well for me. He's spicy, like thyme or rosemary. I don't think I've met anyone before, or since him, who can smell delicious and so fucking masculine all at once. I've been attracted to this man since I was nineteen years old. I remember what he looks like naked.

Dear sweet Jesus, he's seen *me* naked.

I never should have agreed to this.

"Do you want some more?" Kat asks with a grin.

"More what?"

"Wine. You sucked that down like a champ."

I frown down at my glass and set it away from me. "Oh. No. But it's five o'clock somewhere, right?"

"That's my philosophy," Cami says with a nod.

"So, I know this is going to be a competition show," Camden says, pulling me back to the task at hand. "But I don't have many of the specifics."

"Well, it's not going to be a surprise show," Trevor says. "I'm not going to throw lemon peel and mushrooms your way, and demand that you make it into a masterpiece in fourteen minutes."

"Okay," Camden says with a nod. "How will this work?"

"I want you and Mia to do some brainstorming on recipes. Dishes that are a challenge, but fun to watch you make. If you have signature dishes you're known for, or if you have a specific recipe coming up in your new cookbook, that would be fantastic. For this pilot episode, we'll do five recipes and then choose our favorite three for the actual show."

"What are they competing for?" Cami asks and sips her water. Her blue eyes are full of humor as she looks back and forth between us. "Fame? Fortune? Their own cooking show?"

"They already have those," Trevor replies with a laugh. "I was thinking bragging rights."

"That's boring," Addie says with a frown. She tucks her blonde hair behind her ear, then taps her lips in thought. "Maybe they can win a certain amount of money to be donated to their favorite charity?"

"I like that," I reply with a nod. "Neither of us needs money." I look to Camden for confirmation. He doesn't say anything, just holds my gaze and nods in agreement. "We should make donations to a charity. We can switch it up each week."

"That's a good idea," Kat says with a nod, and Trevor makes notes in his notebook.

"Will we be cooking at the same time?" I ask.

"Yes. You'll be using the same kitchen together."

"How do we know that Mia won't cheat?"

My head whips up in surprise, but Camden is grinning at me.

"I won't have to cheat to kick your ass," I reply.

"You sound confident."

"Cooking is what I do best."

His eyes smolder, just like they used to when he was thinking about sex, and I have to look away from him and turn my attention to Trevor. "What you're saying is, you haven't come up with any recipes yourself? Shouldn't you assign them to us?"

"You just said that cooking is what you do best. I'm not a chef. I want you guys to play with it."

"When do we begin filming?" Camden asks.

"Next Monday."

"A *week* away?" I demand. *That means I have to see Camden for a whole week.*

"That should give you time to decide on recipes and strategy," Trevor says with a nod.

"Surely Camden can't take this much time away from his regular gig," Addie says, and I vow right here and now to bake her brownies every day for the rest of her life.

"I'm free," Camden says with a smile. "My other show has wrapped for the season, so I'm good."

"I don't want to rush this," Trevor says. "And I want the show to succeed."

"Do you and Camden know each other well?" Cami asks. "How did you choose him?"

"I cast him in his current show," Trevor replies.

"Trev and I go way back," Camden confirms. "I think we've been at the network about the same amount of time."

Trevor nods, and I'm still stuck on having to spend time with Camden for a whole week.

"Am I going to have to do this with every competitor for each episode? Spend a week coming up with the menu before we film? That seems . . . *stupid*."

Trevor laughs. "No. We've decided to just focus on this first episode to start and to see how the audience receives it, and then we can work on more shows."

I narrow my eyes at him. "Why do I think you're not telling me the whole truth?"

"I have no idea," Trevor replies.

"I also have to work this week," I remind everyone. "I'll work with Camden, but I still have a kitchen to run."

"I was going to speak to you about that," Cami begins. She's the CPA and money guru of our operation. "We have the budget to hire on some more kitchen help. I think you should consider it."

"No."

"I can help," Camden says and then shrugs when we all stare at him. "I'm here anyway. I've been told that my dishes don't suck."

"You don't know the menu." *I cannot work next to this man every day. I'll climb him like a damn tree after the first day.*

"I can learn."

"Think about it," Addie says. "You don't have to decide now."

"Did no one hear me say no?"

"Grouchy," Riley says between her teeth and I sit back in my seat, staring at her. Her eyes widen and I can hear her thoughts. *Stop being difficult.*

I sigh and resign myself to this weird twist of fate. Camden is back in my life. I never thought that would happen. The culinary world isn't huge, but I've been careful to make sure we haven't crossed paths in all of these years, and now, here we are. Working together.

"I'll think about the offer," I say reluctantly. "We will work in my kitchen this week, but we're filming the show on set."

"Yes," Trevor says. "The set has been made to look exactly like the kitchen here at Seduction."

"I'd like to see your kitchen," Camden says. He may as well have just said he'd like to see me naked. My kitchen is the most intimate part of me.

But I just smile and stand. "This way."

"I'll catch up with you both later," Trevor says.

I walk ahead of Camden, and pray that he's not staring at my ass. I'm a bit heavier than I was when I knew him years ago. Not much, but a bit, and it's all settled in my ass.

"You have a beautiful restaurant," he says from behind me.

"Thank you." I nod and push through the kitchen door, holding it open for him. He stops next to me and takes everything in.

"Clean. Efficient. Top of the line."

"It's all of those things," I agree and give him the tour. I show him the two walk-in refrigerators and freezers. I show him where I keep everything. I avoid looking at him, or touching him.

Especially touching him.

But then it occurs to me. He's *not* avoiding me, and I was the one who left. Shouldn't he be pissed?

"Why are you here?" I ask suddenly and turn to look him in the eye. The expression on his handsome face doesn't change, and for a minute, I don't think he's going to answer me. He's changed so much, and yet, he's exactly the same. He's filled out. His shoulders are wider, his jaw more square. But his eyes are the same.

"I don't know," he finally says. "My first reaction was to turn Trevor down, especially when he told me I'd be working with you."

I nod. "Seems logical."

"But then I thought about it, and I decided that I wanted to see you. And at some point, not today, I'll want to talk to you."

"You're talking to me now."

He raises a brow. Perfectly, of course. "You know exactly what I'm talking about."

"Look—"

"Today isn't the day for this conversation," he says. He reaches out to touch my hair and I flinch away. His gaze darkens.

"I don't like to be touched."

"That's new."

I shake my head. "No, it's really not."

"You didn't mind when I touched you."

"You're right."

He steps back and seems to take me in from the top of my head to my feet, and I stand here, wondering if he can see the extra pounds and the extra miles of life that I carry around these days.

"You're as beautiful as you ever were."

I smirk. "Thanks for saying so. You look great. I'm glad you're doing well."

"When do you want to get started?"

"Tomorrow morning. We will have to start early because I have to begin lunch prep at about ten thirty."

"Does seven thirty work?"

"Sure." I cringe inside. That'll mean less sleep for me, but I'll make it work. "I'll meet you here."

"Excellent." He turns to leave, and then stops and looks back at me. "It's good to see you, Mia."

I just nod and then he's gone, and I'm standing in my empty kitchen, alone. How did I let them talk me into this?

"Are you okay?" Addie asks from the doorway. I turn to look at her and shrug.

"Yeah. I think it's still kind of surreal."

She smirks. "I bet. He's handsome. He seems nice, and he looks at you like you hung the moon."

"Please." I shake my head and pull potatoes out of a bin to peel them. "He doesn't even know me."

"He used to," Addie mutters. She looks fantastic, as usual. Addie runs the front of the house, and with a background in fashion she is always put together. She's wearing her glasses today, which only makes her look more mysterious and beautiful.

Kat walks into the kitchen, followed by Riley and Cami.

"Are we having a party?" I ask my business partners.

"A dude you used to be married to just left our restaurant," Cami replies.

"Yes. I was here," I remind her.

"We want to make sure you're good. I can bring you more wine if you need it. I just got a fabulous new Cabernet from France that I've been dying to try."

As our wine bar manager, Kat is excellent in her job. She's also excellent at keeping us liquored up if we need it.

"I have to work," I remind them. "And I appreciate you all being worried about me, but I'm fine. It actually went better than I expected."

"We've known you a long time, Mia," Cami says, narrowing her eyes. "And we have your back. If you're not comfortable with this—"

"I'm *fine*." I sigh and look each of them in the eyes. They're my best friends, my business partners, and they know me better than anyone else. "Honest."

"Okay." Kat nods. "Let's get out of her kitchen before she throws a potato at us."

"Good plan," I agree and shift my focus to peeling potatoes.

"But you'll tell us if you're ever *not* okay?" Riley asks.

"Sure." I plaster a smile on my face and make a shoo motion with my hand. "Now get the hell out of my kitchen."

"She's so bossy," Cami says as they all file out of the kitchen, and I'm left with my own thoughts.

I saw Camden today, and it didn't kill me.

Yet.

Chapter Two

~Camden~

$\mathcal{I}$ come to Portland often. It's a foodie's paradise, and I enjoy visiting a few times a year. I've known that Mia lives here, and I'd heard through the restaurant grapevine that she'd opened her own place. Until today, I haven't visited it. It seemed respectful to stay away. Mia made it clear years ago that she was moving on with a life that didn't include me. Showing up at her restaurant just seemed like a douche move in the past.

But when the job offer came in for this gig, I was torn between wanting to jump at it and turning it down flat.

Then, late one night with only my insomnia and fuzzy brain, I replied to Trevor's email and accepted the job.

I've had relationships since Mia. None that lasted long, and none that I would have considered taking to the 'til death do we part phase. Having just ended a brief relationship, I thought it might be time to see her face to face. To talk to her, and to see if the chemistry is still there.

I'm no expert, but I'd say it's still there. She's beautiful. I couldn't stop looking at her, listening to her voice.

It's like I'd been in the desert for a week and she was a cool drink of water.

"Well?" my sister, Stephanie, asks as I walk into the vacation rental we have for the week. "How was it?"

"It was"—I tilt my head—"interesting."

I walk past her to the kitchen and retrieve a bottle of water from the fridge just as my brother-in-law, Chip, returns from a run around the neighborhood. He's panting, and sweaty, and steals my water for himself.

Knowing that I'd be in town for a while, I rented this house rather than stay in a hotel. Steph and Chip live up in Seattle and came down for the week to relax. Now that I live in L.A. full time, I don't see them as often as I'd like.

"Thanks," Chip says with a grin. I reach for another and snap the top off, take a long drink, and smile at my sister.

"Talk," she demands.

"There's not much to say," I reply and lean my hips against the countertop. "It was just an initial meeting, I got the tour, and we start working tomorrow morning."

"That's not what I want to know."

"I feel good about it," I answer, deliberately avoiding any talk of Mia.

"That's not what I want to know either."

Chip rolls his eyes and kisses his wife on the forehead. "Leave the man alone."

"No," she says and props her hands on her hips. She's in full-on big sister mode. "Tell me about her."

"Who?"

Chip laughs and tosses his empty bottle in the recycle bin.

"I'm going to throat punch you," Steph says with narrowed eyes.

"You're so violent." I smirk and then shrug. "She looks great. The restaurant is pretty amazing. It's a fresh, fun concept with the aphrodisiacs on the menu and the atmosphere is romantic. They've done a really great job."

"And?"

"And what?"

"Is she single?"

I scowl at her. "I didn't ask. And that's not what I'm here for, Steph. I'm here to work."

"And to check her out," Steph replies.

"I never should have told you that I was doing this show with her."

"You're right," Chip says with a nod. "You know how nosy your sister is."

"I'm not nosy," she insists. "He's my baby brother, and I've taken care of him all by myself since he was a teenager."

"I'm not a teenager now," I remind her and then wrap my arms around her to give her a hug.

"I might be a little nosy," she admits.

"I admit I wanted to see her." I pull back and shrug. "There's still chemistry there. But I can tell that she's *not* interested in anything personal."

"How can you tell?" Steph asks.

"She's cold. Distant. Didn't even want to look me in the eyes."

She rolls her eyes. "Men can be so dumb. You made her uncomfortable, given the circumstances, but that doesn't mean she's not interested. You don't know her, and she doesn't know you anymore. If you don't want anything personal between you, do the show and walk away. And she can do the same. No harm, no foul. But if you spend some time together, and you fall in love, well . . . that's pretty cool. I want to be in the wedding."

"Hold on there, fast girl." I shake my head. "No one is talking about love."

"Least of all, you," she replies, making me frown.

"I'm going to end this conversation." I take a drink of water. "I'm going to Seduction tonight for dinner. You're both welcome to join me if you want."

"Is that even a question?" Steph asks Chip. "Does he honestly think that I *don't* want to go?"

"He's not stupid," Chip says with a laugh. "We're in, bro."

"It'll be good to see her again," Steph says. "Does she look the same?"

No, she's sexier than I remember.

"Pretty much."

"She's such a pretty girl," she says.

"I thought we changed the subject."

"You did," Chip says. "My wife is going to be talking about this all week."

"You don't have to stay," I say immediately, making them both laugh. "It was good to see you."

"I'm on vacation," she reminds me with a wink. "And I'm excited to eat at Mia's place tonight."

I nod and leave them, closing myself up in my bedroom. I need to think about some recipe ideas for tomorrow. I need to *not* think about how long Mia's hair is, or how her curves filled out the T-shirt she was wearing. I definitely shouldn't think about how amazing and soft her skin looked.

And when she laughs, I just can't take my eyes off her.

Accepting this project might be the worst mistake of my life. I thought I was over her. Hell, I *am* over her. But not even two minutes after seeing her again I wanted to strip her naked and fuck her senseless.

The sex between us was always amazing.

But now, I have to keep my hands to myself and be professional.

I take a deep breath and then laugh at myself. How could I possibly be so attracted to a woman who left me without a backward glance ten years ago? She didn't even say goodbye in person. She was just *gone*.

I need some answers to questions I've carried for ten years. And I'll get them. I'll do the show, and then I'll move on.

Easy.

"OH, YOU WERE right," Steph says later that night after we're seated at our table. "This place is beautiful."

I nod and glance around. The lighting is low, and each table has flameless candles burning. The booths against the walls are tucked behind heavy curtains, giving couples an intimately cozy experience.

The artwork is provocative and all originals by local artists.

Just like the name of the place suggests, it's sexy.

"It's good that we had reservations," Chip says.

"And it's a Wednesday," Steph adds. "That's unusual."

"Trevor says it's like this every night," I reply as I read the menu. It's not a huge menu, but it's diverse and has something for just about everyone. The waitress returns to take our order, and I decide on the swordfish.

After our meals arrive, and after just a few bites, I see Mia come out of the kitchen to take a quick trip through the dining room. She's stopping at tables to say hello, and I assume to make sure that the food is satisfactory. She smiles at each individual person, laughs with them, and even stops to have a conversation.

"She does look great," Steph says with a grin.

Mia's long, dark hair is pulled up under her white chef's hat. She's in the white coat and dark pants, but she makes it look sexier than fuck.

"She's okay," I reply and smile. "If you like that sort of thing."

"He likes that sort of thing," she informs Chip.

"I'll be back."

"You'll miss saying hello to Mia," Steph says. "You came here to see her."

"I don't want to make her uncomfortable."

Steph rolls her eyes and I stand to walk to the restroom. I don't know why I don't want to talk with her tonight. I'm still getting my bearings where she's concerned, and my sister is too observant. I wanted to see her in action, and I wanted to taste her food. I didn't know that she'd make the rounds through the dining room.

I take a quick trip to the restroom, and on my way out almost run right into Addison.

"Well, hi Camden," she says with a big smile. "I saw your name on the reservation list. How is everything?"

"It's great. You have a fantastic place here, Addie."

"We do," she agrees, nodding her head. "Is that your sister?"

I look over my shoulder, following Addie's gaze. "Yes, that's Stephanie and her husband Chip."

"Mia must have said something funny."

Both Steph and Mia are laughing loudly, their heads tossed back. Mia touches Steph's shoulder, and that sets my teeth on edge.

"She said she doesn't like to be touched," I murmur.

"She's not being touched, she's touching. That's different," Addie replies and pats my shoulder. "She obviously likes your sister."

"They've met before."

Addie just nods. "She's one of the best people I know."

I turn my attention back to her. "My sister?"

"No, *my* sister. I don't remember a time in my life when I didn't have Mia in it. If that's not the same as being sisters, I don't know what is. She has her defenses up, and it's not easy for her to trust. She's stubborn, and she works too hard. But she's also loyal almost to a fault, and when she loves you, she loves so completely that your life will never be the same."

"Why are you telling me this?"

"I don't know," she says with a shrug. "I guess I can just see the way you look at her. None of us know exactly what happened between you years ago. She doesn't speak of it. Ever."

I turn to look at Mia again and feel my heart pound harder.

"And she'd be pissed if she knew I was saying any of this. So, I'll just end with this. She's so *good*, Camden. And I don't want to see her hurt."

"Me either."

She nods and walks away, and I stop to look at the woman in question again. She's still talking to Steph and Chip. Her cheeks are flushed from the hot kitchen. Her blue eyes are happy. There's one stray piece of hair that's escaped from the back of her hat.

I want to twist that hair around my finger.

I walk back over and take my seat.

"What's so funny?"

"Oh, nothing," Mia says, waving me off. "How is everything?"

"This fish is a little dry."

Her eyes narrow on me, and I can't help but laugh. "I'm kidding. It's delicious."

"Be nice," Steph says. "Why are men such shits?"

"Good question," Mia says. "Don't forget to call me. I'd love to chat with you."

"Oh, I won't forget," Steph promises. Mia nods and moves on to the next table.

"What was that all about?"

"I'd forgotten how funny she is," Steph says and takes a bite of her spaghetti. "This is the best red sauce I've ever had."

"I thought mine was the best you've ever had," I reply.

"That was before I had this. Sorry." She shrugs a shoulder. "She does look great. Maybe a little tired."

I noticed.

"So, you're going to call her?"

She takes another bite and then nods. "Yeah, I think I'll see if she wants to get pedicures or something."

"Why?"

She stares at me and then takes another bite of her food.

"Because I like her."

I nod.

"Do you *not* want me to see her?"

"I don't mind either way."

"I think he's lying," she says to Chip, who's been wise and had food in his mouth constantly through this conversation. He just shrugs one shoulder and takes another bite of his steak.

"Why would you care if I spent a couple of hours with Mia?"

"I don't care."

She sighs and takes a sip of wine. "I like her, Camden. We're adults. We can be friends. There doesn't have to be any drama."

"Am I causing drama?" I ask Chip, who just shakes his head, still chewing.

"I have a question for you," Steph says.

"Oh, good." I roll my eyes and snag another piece of bread. Mia always made excellent bread.

"What do you think of her?"

"I don't know her, remember?"

"Knowing what you do. What do you think?"

"She's intelligent, an excellent chef—"

"Jesus H Christ, Camden, answer the fucking question."

"She's amazing. Is that what you want to hear? She's a stellar chef. She's smart and beautiful. That was never a question. I've known that she's amazing for years, and seeing her today only cements that fact. What do you want from me?"

"That," she replies with a smile. "Just that."

I DIDN'T SLEEP much last night. That's nothing new. I rarely sleep for longer than three hours at a time. But I didn't sleep *at all* last night. I kept thinking about Mia. How she looks, what she said, how I feel about her.

I shouldn't feel *anything* about her. She's a colleague, and I'm pretty sure the statute of limitations has expired on the whole she-left-me-while-I-was-at-work-and-annulled-the-marriage thing. We were young, too young to get married. It was probably all for the best.

But I'm pulled to her in a way that has never happened to me before or since. I'm no saint. There have been women. But never one that I regretted moving on from.

And now, here I am, ten years later, working with this amazing human who can still take the breath from my lungs.

I don't know what I want from her, or *if* I want anything at all. But I'm excited to work with her today. We always enjoyed cooking together. It's how we decided to be roommates. My old roomie moved out, and I couldn't afford the place on my own. She was in my culinary program, and needed a place. It seemed logical and convenient.

We were partners in class, and knew we got along well. But what I didn't consider was that not only is Mia *fun* to work with, she's sexy as fuck when she cooks. I couldn't keep my hands off her.

That's something that I'll have to work on. I don't need a sexual harassment suit.

The thought makes me grin as I walk into the Starbucks down the street from Seduction. If there's one thing that I remember about Mia, aside from how it feels to be next to her when she's naked, it's that she's one grouchy person before coffee. Maybe she's already had some, but coming in with backup can't hurt.

It's just seven fifteen when I arrive. I'm early, but Cami is coming out of the front door. She smiles when she sees me.

"Hi," she says.

"Good morning. I'm early."

"Well, Mia's in the kitchen. I just had to finish up some payroll stuff, and my computer at home finally gave up the ghost, so I came into the office. Employees still have to get paid."

I nod and she points at the coffee. "For Mia?"

"It is."

"Going in with ammo. You're smart."

"She likes coffee."

She nods. "She's not really a morning person."

"Are you trying to warn me?"

"It's never a bad thing to have all of the information."

"True."

She tilts her head and props her hands on her hips, watching me. "How long were you together? Before?"

"She didn't tell you?"

She simply shakes her head no.

"A few months."

"Did you love her?"

I frown, and she shakes her head. "Forget I asked. I'm nosy by nature, especially when it comes to my girls. She's important to me."

It's like talking to Addie last night.

"I'm just here for a job, Cami. And I have a soft spot for Mia. I'm not a jerk."

"Are you sure?"

"I don't recall ever being called a jerk," I reply honestly. "And it's not my intent to hurt anyone's feelings. I don't want to talk about our past with you if she hasn't already told you herself."

"I get that," she says and holds up her hands in surrender. "And I even approve of that. It means you have integrity, and I respect it. No need to tell me secrets. I just wanted to point out that she can be tough to work with, but it just means that she wants everything to be perfect."

"Well, then she and I are on the same page there."

Cami grins. "Go on in. I'll lock the door behind you. Have a good morning."

"You too."

I walk past her, through the empty restaurant to the kitchen. The door is propped open, and music is playing from a wireless speaker on the counter. Adele is setting fire to the rain and Mia is moving her hips back and forth as she puts dry goods away, her back to me.

She's wearing a sweatshirt Flashdance-style, exposing one perfect shoulder. She's in black leggings and sandals with a closed toe.

Her curly black hair is piled on top of her head in a messy bun, and I want nothing more than to shake it loose and grab it tightly, just the way she likes it, while I—

"You're early."

I shake my head, clearing my thoughts and look into her blue eyes.

"I'm always early."

"Hmph." She walks into the freezer and then comes out with a big pan full of roast. "I need to prep this and get it in the oven."

"French dips for lunch?"

"It's the special," she replies. "It'll take me five minutes, and then I'll have time for you."

"I can help."

"Not necessary."

I move next to her and she glares up at me. "No means no, Camden."

My lips twitch and I can't help but touch the end of her nose with my finger. "You're still not a morning person."

"I have knives," she replies. "Lots of knives."

"So noted."

Her eyes zero in on the coffee. "Is that for me?"

"It is."

She stops and turns away from the beef.

"Is it an Americano?"

"Right again."

She sighs. "God damn it."

"What's wrong?"

"You brought me coffee."

"You like coffee."

"Yeah, and you're going to make me be nice to you, and that wasn't part of the plan."

I chuckle and pass the cup to her. "I'm a likeable guy."

She takes a sip, considering me.

"You're okay."

I raise a brow.

"Thank you for the coffee."

"You're welcome."

"Now go away so I can do this. Being watched makes me nervous."

"And you've agreed to be on TV?" I cock a brow and she narrows her eyes on me.

"Yes, smarty pants, because it's what's best for the restaurant."

I take a sip of my coffee, watching her sip her own, taking her in.

"I've watched you cook dozens, if not hundreds, of dishes."

"It made me nervous then too," she mutters, surprising me.

"Why didn't you say anything?"

She shrugs that bare shoulder, and my cock twitches. Damn it, maybe it's best if I don't watch her cook.

So, I turn and walk out of the kitchen. I need more coffee. And a fucking cold shower.

Chapter Three

~Mia~

*H*ow am I going to do this? He's been here for five minutes, and I feel unfocused and just . . . *ridiculous.*

He brought me coffee, and he remembered the way I order it from Starbucks. How could he possibly remember that? He can't be nice to me. I won't survive this if he's nice. He'll bring me coffee, and maybe flirt with me a little, and then he'll leave after the taping, and I'll be sad. It's just stupid.

"Get a grip," I mutter to myself and set the heavy pan of roast beef in the oven to slow roast for the lunch crowd.

I walk out to the dining room, but it's empty. Of course, *now* I'm ready for him, and he's nowhere to be found. "Camden?" Maybe my morning bitch-show scared him off for good. It's probably for the best.

I march back into the kitchen and begin chopping vegetables for salad. It's usually the sous chef's job, but I'm here now, so I might as well work.

Unfortunately, with no sleep and only one cup of coffee in me, I'm not as focused as I should be, so I work slower, sure to not cut myself. I've worked many a night with a cut hand, and it sucks balls, so I avoid it at all costs.

With the veggies chopped, I turn to fetch the ingredients for the house-made dressings, and suddenly another cup of Starbucks is under my nose.

Thank God for Addie.

"Oh, I love you," I murmur and take the cup, then a long sip.

"I had no idea that Starbucks was all it would take to hear those words from you."

I spin and stare in horror at Camden.

"I thought you left."

"Clearly we both needed more coffee before we tried to kill each other."

I narrow my eyes and take another sip. "I don't know what you're talking about. I'm a fucking delight in the morning."

He chuckles and crosses his arms over his chest, leans against the countertop and smiles at me. "You're certainly beautiful in the morning."

I blink slowly. "Yes, looking homeless is all the rage these days."

His eyes do that damn smolder thing they do when he's thinking sexy thoughts. "You don't look homeless. You look rumpled."

"Stop." I point my finger at him. "It's too early for your smolder."

"My what?"

"You know what. And it's too early for it. We need to get to work."

"Are you going to always be this bossy?"

"Yep." I smile brilliantly and grab a notebook. "Let's go sit at a table."

We grab our coffees and settle into a booth. I'm across from him now, with a table between us, but he's still got that smolder on his face. I ignore it, and do my best to remain professional.

"Have you given any thought to dishes you'd like to do?" I concentrate on the paper, writing *Mia* on one side and *Camden* on the other, then draw a nice, thick line between the two names.

"You always liked lists."

"Lists are an imperative part of life. Without lists, you'd forget everything you have to do, and we can't have that."

"No, we can't have that. Stop biting your lip."

I glance up in surprise. "I wasn't."

"You were." He shifts in his seat and rubs his fingertips over his forehead. "Let's hear your ideas first."

"Okay." I set the pen down and rub my hands together. "I'd like to do one fish dish. Maybe salmon. I think fish is something that a lot of people are intimidated by because it's delicate and it's easy to screw it up, but we can show them easier ways to make a delicious piece of fish."

"I like that," he says with a nod, so I write *fish* under my name on the list.

"Now your turn."

"Cajun chicken alfredo," he says immediately.

"Oh, that sounds wonderful."

"It is," he agrees with a nod. "I learned it from this old guy just outside of Baton Rouge. It's fantastic."

"On the list," I murmur and write *Cajun alfredo Goodness* under Camden's name. "I think it would be fun to do a quirky appetizer. Like a—"

"I have an amazing stuffed mushroom recipe with chorizo that's pretty amazing."

"I have one, too, but I use an Italian sausage. We could both do them, with our different recipes, and viewers can make the one that looks best to them."

"I like it," he says with a nod. "And we can try each other's on camera too and give feedback."

"That's a good idea. As a viewer, I love it when chefs do that. It makes me want to make the recipe even more."

"I agree."

"Who's going to judge the dishes?" I ask. "I don't think Trevor mentioned that."

"No, he didn't. I'm not sure."

"This is fun." I do a little shimmy in my seat and write *stuffed mushrooms* under both of our names. "Let's do two more."

"I think it would be fun to use a grill. We could do a BBQ dish, or even something as simple as burgers, with our own twist to them."

"Have you tried the burgers with the cheese *inside* of them?"

He blinks for a second, gathering his thoughts. "Yes."

"It should be illegal," I reply. "I like the grill idea. Let's add it."

I write *yummy grill* under our names.

"Have you honed your dessert skills over the past ten years?" he asks with a grin.

"I always made good desserts."

"I seem to remember a situation with a smoky apartment, fire alarms and burnt brownies. The fire department showed up."

"That wasn't my fault," I counter. "If you hadn't talked me into getting naked, I wouldn't have—" I stop and sit back, frowning down at my notebook.

"You wouldn't have what?"

"Nothing." I shake my head and write *dessert* under my column. "I make some signature desserts we can decide on later."

I move to climb out of the booth, but he puts his hand on my arm, stopping me cold.

"What?"

"What just happened?"

"Look, Camden, I think we're going to have fun cooking together. We always did before, there's no reason that we won't now. But we don't really need to rehash all of the *good ol' days*. And you can just back off with the smolder, too."

"I don't have a smolder," he says, frustration hanging heavily in his voice. "I was trying to have a fun conversation with you. We're going to be working together on national television. It's not going to work if it looks like you hate me during the whole thing."

"I *don't* hate you."

"No?"

"No."

"Then why the attitude?"

"I don't have an attitude. But if you'd like to see one, I'm sure I can oblige."

"Jesus, you're difficult," he mutters and rubs his hands over his whole face this time.

"I can turn on Susie Sunshine for the cameras," I reply. "And I'm not trying to be a bitch. I'm really not. But there's no need to talk about before."

Between his smolder and hashing out the past, it's going to be impossible to remain professional. I'm so damn drawn to him, and that's not what we're here for.

That's not the plan. Not to mention, he never said he wants me. I refuse to embarrass myself with this man. So the more distant I am, the better.

"Oh, we're going to talk about it," he replies grimly.

"I have to get in the kitchen."

"I know. But you can't run away every time I see you, and we will talk. But it won't be here."

"Hi pot, I'm kettle. I seem to remember seeing you run off to the restroom when I made my way to your table last night."

His hands fist on the table and he takes a deep breath.

"That wasn't the same."

"Okay." I roll my eyes and move to stand again, but he holds me back again.

"We'll talk, Mia."

"Well, I don't plan to see you outside of here, so—"

He just grins, and I know I've lost this little argument.

"Are you having a nice time with your sister?" I ask, trying to change the subject.

"It's good to see her," he says with a nod. "You seem to get along well."

"She was always nice to me."

"Does *she* get to talk about the past with you?"

"*She* hasn't brought it up," I reply. *Besides, she never saw me naked.*

"Hmm," he says. "She and Chip are down on vacation for the week. I think we're having dinner on the river this evening, if you'd like to join us."

Hell no.

"Thanks, but I'll be working."

"Do you work every day?" he asks.

"Not *every* day."

"When was your last day off?"

I frown, thinking, but I can't remember. "It was probably a week ago."

"That's a lie," he says easily. "You can't remember."

"If you're so fucking psychic, why are you asking me questions?"

"Why are you so on edge?"

I take a deep breath so I don't throat punch him. I'm on edge because *he* puts me on edge. And he does it without even trying. "Have a nice dinner tonight."

I stand and gather my notebook.

"Oh, and thanks for the coffees, too."

"Shall we start cooking tomorrow morning?"

I nod, resigned to never sleeping again. "Same time."

"I'll be here."

"See you then."

I walk back to my kitchen and start making a list of extra ingredients that I'll need to order for these recipes. I'm not working tonight, but I can't spend time with Camden outside of this project. I'm still ridiculously attracted to him, and I'll make a fool of myself.

I already did that once with him. I won't do it again.

My phone buzzes with a text from Cami. *Don't forget dinner tonight at our house. 6:00.*

I smile and reply. *I'll be there. What can I bring?*

The dots blink on the phone as she replies. *A bottle of red. I have the rest covered.*

You got it.

Spending the evening with my best friend and my brother is much less likely to end in catastrophe than if I'd accepted Camden's invitation.

"Oh God, I'm so full," Cami says as she unbuttons the top of her jeans and lounges back in her chair on the patio.

"It was good," I reply.

"Why do you sound surprised?" Landon, my brother, asks. "I can cook, you know."

"I'm not surprised. I am, however, hopeful that I'll still be alive tomorrow."

"Har har," he says, then plants a kiss on Cami's cheek. "How was your day?"

"Long," I reply with a yawn. "I didn't sleep last night, and had to be in my kitchen at about seven this morning to start working with Camden, so I'm tired."

"How did that go?" Cami asks.

"Fine." I shrug. "He's nice enough."

"Are you ever going to tell us what happened?" Cami asks. "We've tried to be patient and wait until you offer the information, but I think you have top-level security clearance with the CIA because getting information out of you is impossible."

"I could tell you, but then I'd have to kill you," I reply with a sassy wink.

"I have security clearance with the navy, so you can tell me," Landon says. His voice sounds like he's being funny, but his eyes are hard. "He hurt you, didn't he? I'm going to have to kill him and make it look like an accident."

Scoot, Cami's cat, comes out onto the patio and jumps up onto the chaise next to Landon. He curls up and purrs loudly.

I frown and shake my head. "He didn't really do anything wrong."

Neither of them replies, they just sit quietly, watching

me. Maybe it's time I talk about it in detail with *someone*, rather than just give out bits and pieces. I'm not going to have a more supportive audience than my best friend and my brother.

"Camden and I went to culinary school together up in Seattle. He was *so hot*. I mean, you've seen what he looks like now, and to be honest he's gotten hotter, but at about twenty, he was just—"

"I can only imagine," Cami says with a wink. "He's a hottie."

"Hey," Landon says.

"You're a hottie too, babe," she says and kisses his shoulder. "Keep talking."

"We were lab partners, so we worked together in the kitchen about three times a week. We worked well together. We laughed a lot, and he was just a nice guy."

"He sounds horrible," Cami says with a wink.

"Yeah, it was tough." I sigh and stand, not able to sit anymore, and pace the big patio. "One day, he came into class and looked stressed out. Turns out, his roommate had to suddenly move out. So that meant that Camden was left without a roommate, and he was worried that he'd have to quit school because he couldn't afford it all himself."

"So, he doesn't come from a wealthy family," Landon says.

"No. In fact, both of his parents were killed when he was young, like maybe around twelve I think? And his older sister Stephanie raised him."

"Wow," Cami says. "That's sad."

"Anyway, at about that same time, the house that I was

renting with a couple other girls was being sold out from under us, so we needed to find a new place."

"I remember that," Cami says.

"I don't remember any of this," Landon says with a scowl.

"You were off being a sexy pilot," Cami replies, waving him off.

Scoot jumps off the chaise and begins to follow me around the patio as I pace.

"So, when he told me that he needed a roommate, I said I did too, and it made sense to just move in together."

"Wait. You were dating him?" Cami asks.

"No. We were just friends."

"Okay," she says with a nod. "Just clarifying."

"It was a two-bedroom apartment, not far from the school. He already had all the furniture, so it was great because all I had was my personal stuff. We got along well." I grin and then feel myself blush. "Really well, actually. After I moved in, and we were spending more time together, he couldn't keep his hands off me."

"I don't want to know this part," Landon says, but Cami hushes him.

"I do. I really do. Keep talking."

"Now, I need to clarify that we never said we were girl-friend and boyfriend. He never said the L word. Ever. But we fucked all the damn time."

"Atta girl," Cami says as Landon continues to scowl.

"So, there was chemistry and good sex and I truly believe we were also good friends. We watched a lot of movies, practiced recipes, and just generally hung out."

"He was totally your boyfriend," Cami says.

"I was so insecure," I reply with a sigh. "You remember, Cami. If you think I have insecurities now, it's nothing compared to then. I was overweight, and kids are horrible. *Boys* were horrible. And suddenly, this super-hot guy wanted me." I turn and stare at Cami, just as confused now as I was then. "Why did he do that?"

"Because he was hot for you," Landon says. "Because he's not an asshole and knows that women come in all shapes and sizes, and you're an amazing girl."

"All of that," Cami says with a nod. "Also, I want to marry you all over again."

"I'm not done," I remind them. "So, after we'd been living together for maybe three or four months, I missed a period."

"Oh God." Cami covers her mouth with her hands.

I nod. "I didn't mention it for a few days, hoping that I would just start, but I didn't. So I told him, and he wasn't freaking out. Not like I thought he would. He just went out and bought a pregnancy test."

"Oh my God," Cami says again.

I swallow hard and stand with my back to them, looking out on their backyard.

"It was positive. That was on a Thursday evening. I called the doctor the next day, but they couldn't get me in until Tuesday. I was so fucking scared. I didn't know what to do. I didn't want him to think that I was trying to trap him into being with me. That's just stupid."

I turn back to face them again.

"And we weren't technically a couple. He'd never said I

love you. And neither did I, to be honest. But he decided, right then and there, that we were getting married."

"What?" Landon demands.

"Yeah. I know. Dumb. But we were twenty, and he said he was going to do the right thing. We got all caught up in the idea of it all, and the next thing I knew, we were standing in the courthouse, signing a marriage license and got married on the spot."

"You got fucking *married*?" Landon yells.

"Don't yell at me now, you idiot; it was ten years ago, and I'm not married anymore." I roll my eyes and pace some more. "So I went to the doctor on that Tuesday, and it turned out that I *wasn't* pregnant."

"You lost the baby?" Cami asks.

"No. I was never pregnant. It was a false positive. I didn't know what the fuck to do. He only married me because I was pregnant, and I *wasn't* pregnant. So, I went back to the apartment and packed my things and left."

"You didn't even talk to him?" Landon asks.

"I left him a note that basically said that I wasn't pregnant and now he could go find someone to love for real. I came back to Portland and went to school here."

"Did you ever hear from him again?"

"Not until the other day when he walked into our bar." I take a deep breath and look up to find them staring at me like I'm a complete moron. "What?"

"So, you just left, and didn't try to have an adult conversation with the man?" Landon asks and I suddenly feel so foolish.

"I'm a horrible human being." I cover my eyes and fight the tears that want to come. "But to be fair, he didn't chase after me. But yes, I'm horrible."

"No, you were twenty. And scared," Cami says. "You were upset and afraid of being rejected by him."

"I truly thought that the baby was the only reason he married me."

"Well, that may be true," Landon says. "But he definitely cared about you. If he wasn't into you and the relationship, he would have had an entirely different reaction when you told him you might be pregnant."

"He's right," Cami says with a nod. "And if you'd called to talk to one of us, we would have told you that."

"I fucked up so bad," I whisper. "I have to apologize. Right now. Tonight."

I head inside the house, and Cami and Landon follow me.

"It's almost ten in the evening," Cami says. "This will keep one more night."

"It's already been ten years," Landon reminds me.

"No." I shake my head and grab my bag and keys. "I need to do this *now*."

I rush to the front door and then stop cold.

"What's wrong?" Cami asks.

I turn to her and let the tears fall. "I don't know where he's staying."

"Aw, sugar, you're tired." Landon wraps his arms around me and hugs me close. I haven't let anyone get this close to me physically in a long time, and it feels so good. "You can talk to him in the morning."

"Yeah." I sniffle and wipe my nose on his shirt.

"Did you just do what I think you did?"

"You're still hugging me," I reply, as if that explains it all. "You get what you get."

"You really are a horrible human being," he says.

"I know." I sigh and finally hug him back. "I'm a bad person."

"It's okay." Cami pats my back. "We're still keeping you."

Chapter Four

~Camden~

I don't know why I'm pounding on the restaurant door for the sixth time. No one answered the first five times, so the likelihood of them answering now is, well, unlikely.

It's almost eight, and Mia's still not here. Of course, I don't have her number. I'll be rectifying that situation today.

In the meantime, where the fuck is she?

I pace on the sidewalk. Traffic is heavy now with people scrambling to get to work. I've almost been trampled twice by speed walkers, so I lean against the brick wall and sip my coffee.

Mia's is getting cold.

When she doesn't arrive by eight, I call Trevor.

"Mia's not here," I say when he picks up the phone. "She should have been here a half hour ago. Can you please call her?"

"Of course. I'll call you right back."

I end the call and narrow my eyes as I take another long sip of black coffee. This is unlike Mia, and it sets me on edge.

Which is stupid.

My phone rings.

"Hello."

"She didn't pick up," Trevor says with a sigh. "Oh wait." He mumbles something to Riley. "Give me a few more minutes, Camden."

And with that, he hangs up. What in the hell is going on? Is she okay?

Just when I'm about to call Trevor again, he calls me.

"Yeah."

"Sorry, man. She's okay. She should be there in less than an hour."

"Thanks for letting me know."

I walk over to the Starbucks to get another coffee for me and a fresh one for her. The line is long at this time of day, so by the time I get back to Seduction, Mia is just running up to the front door, her keys clutched in her hands.

"I'm so sorry," she says breathlessly. She unlocks the door and ushers me in, then locks it again behind us and walks quickly toward the kitchen. Her hair is still down around her shoulders, and her cheeks are flushed, the way they used to be after I'd fucked her senseless.

"I'm so, so sorry," she says again and turns to look at me. "I overslept. I *never* do that. Is that coffee for me?"

"Under one condition," I reply and pass my phone to

her. "Put your number into my phone and you can have the coffee."

"You're holding the coffee hostage for my phone number?"

"Yes."

Her eyes dance with humor as she accepts my phone and punches in her number then hands it back. "Gimme."

She takes a sip of her hot drink and sighs. "It wouldn't have made a difference if you had my phone number today or not. I forgot it last night."

"Here?"

She frowns. "No."

She was with a dude. Of course. She's successful and beautiful. It makes sense that she would be with someone.

Doesn't mean I don't want to punch the fucker, though.

"I ended up having dinner at Landon and Cami's place, and I forgot my phone when I went home. I slept late. So late, in fact, that I didn't wake up until Landon was standing over me yelling my name."

She turns on the faucet and washes her hands.

"Do you have any idea how mortifying it is to have your brother break into your house to wake you up? Especially when I sleep naked, and it was warm in my house last night, so I didn't have any covers on."

I can't stop the bark of laughter that shoots out of me.

"Yeah, you can laugh, but I think Landon would give his left kidney to be able to rewind the last two hours and have Cami come wake me up."

"Let's go back to the naked part," I say, but she just shakes her head with a laugh. "Seriously. You never used to sleep naked."

"I was twenty," she reminds me with a wink. "That was a while ago."

I tilt my head, watching her. "What else has changed?"

"Only everything," she says with a smile. "Way too much to list right now. I'm seriously very sorry, Camden. This never happens."

"It's not a big deal," I reply with a shrug.

"It sort of is, because now I don't have time to work on our recipes. I haven't done any prep work for the day, so I'm going to have to dig in. And, at some point, I'd like to have a chat with you."

I raise an eyebrow. "Am I in trouble?"

"No." She smiles and reaches for a big bowl. "But we have to save it for later. I have too much—"

Her phone rings, making her frown. "Shit," she mutters before she answers. "Hello. Okay. That's the third time this month." She sighs and rubs her fingers over her eyes, which means she's stressed out. "Fine."

She hangs up and glares at no one in particular.

"What's up?"

"My sous chef just called out sick. Again." She sighs. "Looks like it's just me today."

"You don't have anyone you can call in?"

"Nope. I was already down a chef, and I haven't had time to hire someone. At least I don't have to wash dishes."

"I'll help."

"No."

"Jesus Christ, Mia. I'm obviously qualified and I'm here. I don't have other plans today."

She blows a strand of hair out of her eyes. "Fine. I mean, thank you. First, I need to marinate some chicken for tonight's special." She marches into the fridge and then right back out again with frustration written all over her face.

"My supplier didn't bring the thighs. He brought extra breasts. So I have to shift tracks."

"Suggestion. Let me take care of the special tonight."

"Are you going to the store to get me chicken thighs?"

"No." I list off all of the ingredients for my chicken marsala. "Do you have all of that?"

"Of course."

"It'll be a hit. I promise."

"Should we make a sign saying that you're the guest chef today?" She smirks, but then her eyes widen. "Oh, there could be something to that."

"This is *your* kitchen, Mia."

"Fucking right it is, but if we put on the outside chalkboard that Camden Sawyer is here as a guest chef, it'll pull some people in. Riley would agree with me." She nods decisively.

"I don't give even one shit about my name being anywhere. I'm just trying to take something off your list."

"That's nice of you," she says and gestures to her right. "There are extra aprons and hats in there. You can use that workstation," she nods to the right, "and if you need anything, just ask. I tend to move fast, and I get cranky if people get in my way, but I'll try to rein that in since you're doing me a solid."

God, she's remarkable.

"Sounds good."

She stops and props her hands on her hips. "Are you sure? You don't have to do this."

"It'll be like the good ol' days," I reply, making her roll her eyes. "We always worked well together."

"I guess we should see if that still sticks," she says with a nod. "Okay, here's what I need . . ."

It's two thirty before we have a chance to take any kind of break. The lunch crowd was intense, but Mia moved through it all with complete confidence.

I glance her way and grin. She's shaking her hips, the way she always does when she's stirring something, and turns around to fetch her pepper grinder.

"What?" she asks.

"I'm just watching."

"Why?" She looks at her own butt and then frowns at me. "Do I have something on my ass?"

"No." I reach out and tuck a stray piece of hair behind her ear. "I always did like to watch you cook."

"Well, you're the only one. I'm usually grouchy, but it's just because I want everything to be just perfect, and most of the people I've hired have the shittiest work ethic ever. You're not bad, though."

"Thanks."

She laughs and suddenly wraps her arms around my

middle in a hug. It's over as quickly as it began and she's back at the stovetop before I can say anything.

"I appreciate your help today," she says at last.

"It's been fun. I haven't worked in a restaurant kitchen in about three years, and this reminds me that I miss it."

"Being a big-shot celebrity chef can't suck," she says. Her red bow lips are pursed in a flirty smile and I want to kiss them so bad it hurts.

"You should know," I reply, earning an eye-roll.

"I had one special on TV," she reminds me. "I'm hardly a celebrity."

"Cooking has been good to me," I admit. "I'm doing what I love to do, and it compensates me well."

"That's all any of us wants," she says. "Trevor said the other day that you have a new cookbook coming out?"

"Just before Christmas, yeah," I reply. "They're fun, but a lot of work."

"I can only imagine," she says. "Just coming up with ways to freshen up the menu a few times a year is tough. I can't imagine doing a whole cookbook."

"When does your dinner chef arrive?" I ask.

"You're looking at her."

She walks away from me, into the walk-in freezer this time and when she comes back out carrying five pounds of butter, I take it from her and set it on the countertop.

"Why don't you have more help?" I ask.

"Honestly, it's just easier to do it myself. No one knows my recipes like I do, and they don't taste the same when someone else makes them. It's like someone other than your mom making your favorite childhood dish. It's never the same."

"Mia, you need a day off now and then."

"You sound like everyone else," she says and unwraps the butter. "I'm fine."

"Why did you sleep late today?"

"Camden, I don't have time for your expert psychological analysis today. It may be slower right now, but in about two hours the dinner rush is going to hit, and I won't be able to stop moving until we close the kitchen at ten. I overslept today because I was fucking tired." She turns to me. "That's the truth."

But it's not that simple.

"Okay." I nod and turn back to what I was doing. "I'll need more garlic. Do you have some in the fridge?"

"You don't have to stay for dinner."

"I'm not leaving you here to work by yourself for another eight fucking hours, Mia." She turns to say something but I hold my hand up, stopping her. "The question was about garlic, not whether or not I'm staying."

She glares at me and props her hands on her hips.

"Does that look usually intimidate your employees?"

"Yes."

"I can see that." I nod. "Garlic?"

"Fridge," she says with a sigh. "I'm not paying you for today."

"I'M EXHAUSTED." I take a sip of the red wine that Kat poured for us before she left. The whole place is closed now, and Mia and I are the only ones still here.

"You did great today," she says with a smile. She pulls her hair out of the ponytail and shakes it out until it's framing her face. "That's better."

"We sold out of the special," I inform her with a satisfied grin.

"I heard," she says with a nod. "It was delicious. Thanks again."

"It was fun, but I don't know how you manage to do this every damn day."

"You'd think I would be thinner," she says with a frown and looks down at herself. "But I'm afraid that ship has sailed."

"You're beautiful," I reply.

"You always said that," she says. "I had some pretty intense confidence issues when I knew you, and I always wondered *how* you could find me pretty."

"Why weren't you confident?"

"Because kids and teenagers are mean." She shrugs. "Even my mother used to say, *It's okay, Mia. Italian boys like chubby girls.* She wasn't trying to be mean."

"It sounds mean," I reply and feel my blood heat up. "And for the record, I was attracted to you. Hell, I still am."

Her eyes widen in surprise. "Interesting."

I laugh. "All you have to say is *interesting*?"

"Well, it is interesting. And now that I'm embarrassed, let's keep this train rolling and have that talk I mentioned this morning."

"Okay." I set my wine away from me and turn to face her,

giving her my undivided attention. She looks so damn tired. "What's up?"

"I need to apologize," she says. "And not just about this morning. I was talking with Cami and Landon last night, and for the first time since *before*, I let myself think about everything that happened. I was wrong, Camden.

"I was so fucking embarrassed," she whispers and clenches her eyes shut. "When the doctor told me that the pregnancy wasn't real, I was just mortified. I admit I was also a little sad because even though I was terrified, I didn't hate the idea of the baby. But mostly I was embarrassed. I didn't know what to say to you. We weren't a couple."

I'm hung up on that last sentence. "What?"

"I was embarrassed."

"No, the last thing."

"We weren't a couple?"

"Yeah, that. We weren't? Because I don't think we were on the same page there."

She turns in her seat now, facing me. "Camden, we never said we were an exclusive thing."

"Well I sure as fuck wasn't screwing anyone else. Not to mention, we got *married*, Mia. That's pretty fucking exclusive."

"I wasn't seeing anyone else either." She shakes her head. "I assumed the sex was exclusive, but we never said we were in a relationship. I thought we were friends with some fun benefits."

I sit and let her spill out the rest, but I want to shake her.

"And then we thought I was pregnant, and you shocked the hell out of me when you said we would get married. Before I knew it, we were married. It happened so fast. And then the doctor told me that the only reason you married me wasn't even real."

"The *only* reason?"

"Of course." She frowns and I want to kiss those wrinkles between her eyes. "So, I packed my things and you know the rest.

"I didn't let myself think about you after I came back to Portland. Whenever I did, it only made me sad and so *ashamed*. Instead, I moved ahead and tried to put you in my past."

"Is that it?" I ask. She nods. "I have a few things to say." I take a sip of wine, gathering my thoughts. "First of all, you need to know that I didn't do anything that I didn't want to. You didn't trap me, Mia. You didn't coerce me. I married you because I was excited about the baby."

Her eyes widen in surprise.

"That's right, I was excited. I know that we were too young, and poor as hell, and would have made so many mistakes, but I thought that baby would be an adventure. And going on that adventure with you? Jesus, it doesn't get any better than that. You were my girlfriend. You made me laugh, and you made me think. You challenged me, and that was such a fucking turn-on. So, if you take nothing else from this conversation, remember this: I was there because I *wanted* to be there, not just because it was the *right* thing to do.

"When I got home from work that day and found you gone, well, it was probably one of the worst days of my life, second only to the day my parents died."

She squeezes her eyes closed. "I'm so sorry."

"You could have talked to me. I did some research after you left, and learned that false-positive pregnancy tests happen. We would have discussed it, and decided what to do from there, together.

"Instead, you took that decision and made it yours alone."

"I did," she says with a nod. "And I'm a horrible person."

"No, you're not." I sigh. "Nine years ago, this whole conversation would have made me so fucking mad."

"You know," she says and clears her throat. "You never tried to find me."

"Mia, you made it pretty damn clear that you didn't want to be found."

She nods. "I might have been an overreactor in my youth."

"Maybe a little," I agree. "We were both young and stupid."

"And embarrassed," she reminds me. "Even the doctor told me there were other ways to get a man to stay with me. I didn't have to make up a fake pregnancy."

"That doctor sounds like the stupid one."

She nods, and then shrugs, and drinks the rest of her wine. "I was going to find you last night and apologize. But then I realized that I don't know where you're staying, and I don't have your number."

"You do now."

"I do?"

"I sent you a text earlier."

She frowns. "I haven't even looked at my phone today." She pulls it out of her bag and smiles. "You sent me a cake emoji."

"I was hungry for cake."

"Did you get some?"

I shake my head. "No, the paying customers ate it all."

"How rude," she mutters. "I'll save you a piece tomorrow."

"What time are we coming in?"

"Seven thirty if you want to get any work done."

I frown. "Mia, it's midnight now."

"Yep."

"Let's talk about these workaholic tendencies of yours."

"Or let's not."

"I'm serious. You're going to kill yourself if you keep this schedule up."

"Opening a business is always rigorous, Camden. Of course I put in more than forty hours a week. I have a kitchen to run, and now I've been talked into a television show."

"You didn't want to do the show?" *Why is she doing it if she didn't want it?*

"No way. That was Riley's dream, and once things started happening, it just sort of snowballed. I just wanted to have a successful restaurant. I don't want to be on TV. I'm not exactly TV material."

"That's not the first time you've put yourself down, Mia."

"Oh please." She waves me off. "I'm not putting myself down. I'm stating the truth. There aren't many curvy girls on TV, and that's the truth. Besides, being in front of the camera was never my thing. That's Addie. Yet, here we are. *I'm* the one who gets to be the face of Seduction."

"You're so beautiful," I murmur and reach for her hand. "I wish you believed that."

"I do." She smiles ruefully. "Sometimes. I think self-image issues are part of the girl DNA. I'm not obnoxious about it. But you asked."

"I did?"

"I think so." She laughs now and shrugs. "I don't actually remember."

"If I were to ask you to join me for dinner, somewhere other than Seduction, would you say yes?"

"I don't know. Maybe."

"You have soft hands."

"I wash them a lot."

It's quiet in the restaurant, and the light is low, and in this moment, it feels like we're the only two people in the world. It feels familiar and new all at the same time, and all I know for sure is, I need to kiss her. To have my hands on her.

I stand and lean over her, caging her in between my arms and the bar.

"Mia?"

"Uh huh."

Her eyes drop to my lips and she runs her tongue over her bottom lip, and it's almost my undoing.

"Whether you believe me or not, I think you're the sexiest woman I've ever met."

"Okay."

"And I'm going to kiss you."

Her eyes jump up to meet mine.

"Are you sure that's a good idea?"

"Honestly?" I move between her legs, pressing closer. "I don't give a fuck if it's a good idea. I'm going to do it, and I'm doing it now. So if you're going to say no, you'd better say it now."

"I don't think I'm going to say no."

She takes a deep, shuddering breath and lets it out slowly.

"You should hold on to something," I suggest and immediately regret it when she fists my T-shirt in her hands, holding on tightly. "Ah yes, your old signature move."

"I always had to hold on to something when you kissed me," she whispers.

I brush my nose lightly against hers and move in slowly.

Chapter Five

~Mia~

Jesus, Mary, and Joseph, he's going to kiss me. Maybe he shouldn't have warned me because now all I can think about is that I haven't brushed my teeth in over fifteen hours, and what if he turns his head in the same direction I do and we clash teeth?

Oh God, this could be very bad.

But his hands glide up my arms and into my hair where he fists them and holds on for dear life as his lips sink over mine. He's still for a moment, and then we're all tangled lips and moans of pleasure. It's exactly as I remember it being ten years ago.

His tongue glides over my lips and he nibbles the corner, making the hair on the back of my neck stand on end. He cups my jaw and neck, and peppers sweet kisses over to my cheekbone and farther to my ear.

"So damn sexy," he growls. I can't reply. I'm pretty sure my bones have liquefied, and without him holding me up I'd fall into a puddle on the floor.

That would be a sight for the cleaning crew to behold.

"Did you just laugh?" he asks against my neck. Oh dear Moses, if he kisses my neck I'm done for. Yep. Done for. He pulls my shirt aside and kisses my shoulder too, and I'm pretty sure my vagina is going to explode from hotness overload.

"Maybe," I reply and bite my lip when he nibbles his way back up my neck.

"Why?"

"I don't remember."

He smiles against my lips before he kisses me once more and then pulls away.

"Wow," I whisper. "So you're not impotent after all."

"Excuse me?"

My eyes fly open in horror. "I didn't mean to say that out loud. Ignore that."

"Was there a rumor going around that I'm impotent?"

I silently call myself every horrible name in the book and scrub my hands over my face, trying to pull myself out of the sexual haze Camden just had me in.

"Not that I'm aware of," I reply and clear my throat. "I'm just dumb, and we should never speak of this again."

"If you need me to prove the rumor wrong, I can," he says and I meet his eyes for the first time since the kiss of the century. He's not mad. He's grinning, and if I'm not mistaken, his cheeks are flushed. He's as turned on as I am.

"Maybe another time," I murmur and hop off the stool. He joins me, and I'm thrown by how tall he is. "Did you grow?"

"I don't think so."

"I don't remember you being so tall."

"You're pint-sized," he replies and kisses me on the head.

There's nothing small about me. I don't say it out loud. He doesn't want to hear it, and after that kiss he just planted on me, he clearly gives zero fucks about my size.

"I should go home. It's going to be another early morning."

He's quiet as we both gather our things and I turn out the lights in the restaurant.

"Are you parked over here too?" He's walking next to me down the block toward the parking lot I use.

"No. I'm not going to let you walk down here by yourself at this time of night."

I grin up at him. "That's very chivalrous of you, but I do this every single night."

"You won't while I'm with you." He reaches down and takes my hand in his, linking our fingers.

I suspect that touch is this man's love language. He's a toucher.

I'm the opposite of a toucher.

But I don't pull my hand away. When we reach my car, I unlock it and toss my handbag onto the passenger seat, then turn toward him and catch him checking out my ass.

He doesn't look sorry.

I don't want him to be sorry.

"Take tomorrow night off and go to dinner with me."

"I don't know if you've heard, but I own a business and I'll need to be there."

His lips twitch.

"The world won't fall apart if you take a night off."

"I took a night off last night."

"See? You can make it two nights in one week. The staff won't know what to think."

"Exactly." I shake my head. "I can't be gone two nights in one week."

"Mia." He drags a finger down my cheek. "I want to have you all to myself tomorrow evening."

Damn him for being so persuasive.

"I will leave at seven, after the initial dinner rush."

He sighs. "Compromise is important, I suppose."

I smile and grab his hand before he can pull it away, and press a kiss to his palm. "Thank you."

"But we aren't meeting in the morning," he says firmly.

"Trevor wants—"

"Trevor isn't a chef. You and I both know that we don't need to practice dishes that we've made for years. It's a competition show. We're going to have our own style anyway. You overslept today because you're exhausted, and after watching you work today, although it was sexy as fuck, it's going to kill you. Sleep. I know you'll be at work long before lunch anyway."

"You're awfully bossy. Just because you kissed me doesn't mean you're suddenly in control."

He leans close, his lips inches from mine. "I'm not trying to control you, Mia. I'm trying to take care of you because you're not doing it for yourself. Do me a fucking solid and take the morning off."

"*And* the evening."

"You're working through dinner," he reminds me. He's not angry or frustrated with me. He links his fingers with mine again, holding my hand gently.

"Fine." I sigh and shake my head. "I'll weed my garden in the morning. I think I have some tomatoes ready to pick, and the cucumbers should be close too."

"Tend your garden." He winks at me as I lower myself into my car. "And get some sleep."

"Yes, sir." I give him a mock salute and roll my eyes as I start the car, and roll my window down. "Do you want a ride to your car?"

"I don't think so. I could use a walk."

I nod and wave as I pull away. I watch him in my rear-view mirror, and he stands on the sidewalk, watching me, his hands in his pockets. His hair is disheveled, and I can read his face perfectly.

He wants me.

And for the first time in a long time, I have that fire in my belly that comes with being so damn attracted to a man I can hardly stand it. Camden Sawyer is a sexy, kind, chivalrous man, and I just agreed to take a good portion of the day off tomorrow to be with him.

The girls won't even know who I am when I tell them.

"HOW WAS YOUR morning?" Camden asks after we've ordered dinner. He took me to The Cheesecake Factory, which made me laugh like crazy. Who would believe that two highly skilled chefs would choose The Cheesecake Factory for dinner? We used to love this place back in the day. I still do. The menu is huge, and it's always delicious. Not to mention, you always know what you're gonna get. There aren't any surprises, and as a person who is constantly experimenting and tweaking recipes, it's nice to go back to something you know.

"I slept longer than I expected," I admit and laugh when he cocks a brow. "You can say I told you so."

"No need."

"But I did have time to quickly weed the garden and pick a few things."

"Have you had the garden for a long time?"

"No, actually. I bought the house just before we opened Seduction, so maybe three years ago. I had the kitchen gutted and redone before I even moved in. While that was being finished, I went to the house one day to measure for furniture and stuff, and wandered into the backyard. There was the perfect spot for a small vegetable garden, but with the renovations and getting ready to open the business, there just wasn't time for it.

"This past spring, I decided that Sundays after brunch with the girls would be set aside for the garden."

"You take Sundays off?"

"Mostly." I bite my lip and shrug a shoulder. "Lately, I've been working more. The girls yell at me."

He tips his head to the side and takes a sip of his water. "Yell at you?"

"To take days off," I reply. I check my phone for the third time since we sat down. "I wonder if they remembered that the walk-in freezer door doesn't shut right?"

"Mia?"

"Yeah."

"Put your phone away."

I look up at him and frown. "I have to have it handy in case they need me. What can I say? I'm a workaholic."

"I have a question." He pauses while our meal is delivered, and I immediately dig into my orange chicken. It's *so good*. I should put something like this on our menu. "Do you get off on working?"

I pause, my fork halfway to my mouth. "Excuse me?"

"Does working give you a rush? On your days off, are you itching to go into the restaurant because being away from it is physically painful?"

"That doesn't sound normal."

"You're right, but it's what a workaholic is. I don't believe you're a workaholic."

"You've been around for three days," I remind him with a frown.

"True, and I could be wrong, but from what I've seen so far, you're not a workaholic, you have trust issues."

I frown again, but he puts his hand up. "Let me finish. You said yourself that you don't trust your staff to prepare your dishes the way you've taught them to. You just said that you don't even trust them to shut the freezer door properly.

"You're a control freak, and you want to make sure that everything in your kitchen is *just so*. Which I totally understand. It's your kitchen, and it should be exactly the way you want it. But you should also be hiring people who are competent and have the same work ethic that you do. They should be dependable."

"I haven't found them," I reply, shaking my head. "In the beginning, I tried to do that, and when I'd take a day off, someone would not show up for a shift, or not show up at all. I caught a sous chef who almost send a salad out to a customer who specifically said she was allergic to nuts with almonds all over it."

"Yikes," he says with a cringe.

"Yeah. It's *my* place, and besides the other girls, no one is going to care about it the same way I do. But damn it, Camden, I've build a reputation for this restaurant, and I'm not willing to let these people who could give two shits about it fuck that up for us."

"You love it."

"More than anything else," I agree immediately. "It's my passion. It's everything I ever wanted. So if making sure it's a success means that I don't get many days off, so be it. It's worth it to me."

"You're fucking gorgeous when you talk about it," he says, throwing me completely off. "And when you're working in the kitchen?" He shakes his head and takes a bite of his bread. "It was all I could do not to boost you up on the counter and fuck you brainless."

The couple sitting next to us both look over at us in shock.

"Having a private conversation here, but that's okay. Do

that to her later." Camden suggests to the man, winks at them and I want to crawl under the table and die. "What?"

"Don't try to look innocent," I reply and can't help but giggle.

He leans toward me and cups his hand around his mouth, trying to be all inconspicuous, but he's conspicuous.

"I think she'd enjoy it."

"Stop." I cover my mouth with my hand and try to hold the bubbles of laughter in.

"You'd enjoy it, too," he says and that's it. I can't hold it in anymore. I laugh so hard that tears are streaming down my face. I dab at the corners of my eyes with my napkin and try to pull myself together.

"You're not great for my ego." He's smiling at me as if I'm the most adorable thing he's ever seen.

"There's nothing wrong with your ego."

"There is now that you've had a go at it," he says, but he's laughing with me. *This* is what I missed the most about him. We could talk and laugh for hours.

My phone buzzes with a text, making me frown.

"It's Addie," I say. *You know I don't want to interrupt you, but we want to make sure you're having fun. Do you need me to "create" an issue so you can escape?*

I laugh and reply with, *No, I'm fine. Thank you.*

"Everything okay?" Camden asks.

"Oh yeah." I nod and toss the phone in my bag after all. "Just the girls being girls."

"Offered you a way out of this date?"

I snort and eat the last bite of my meal. "Of course. Okay, back to the conversation at hand. Are *you* a workaholic?"

"I have moments when I am," he says, wiping his mouth as he considers my question. "When we're in the middle of filming, or when I'm researching cookbooks, I immerse myself in it. So I know what that feels like. But I admit that some of it is also the control of it. I want it all to be perfect."

I nod thoughtfully. He gets it.

"Do you want dessert?"

I stare at him, confused. "Do people come to this restaurant and *not* order dessert?"

"Point taken."

We browse the cheesecake menu, and then place an order to go.

"I can't eat it right now," I say and sigh. "I ate *all* the chicken."

"Let's take this back to your place." He pays the waitress and leads me out of the restaurant to his car.

"I'm not getting naked with you tonight," I inform him as I buckle my seat belt. The drive from my house to this restaurant is a long one. I bought a house in an older part of town because I love the neighborhood and the views that come with it. But it's not really close to anything.

"I don't recall asking you to take any of your clothes off."

"I'm just letting you know in advance," I reply and relax into the leather seat of his rental car. "It could get awkward if we're at my place, eating cheesecake, and the next thing I know you're trying to get in my pants and I have to say no. So, I'm saying no now."

"Noted," he says with a nod. "No getting your pants off today. What about your shirt?"

I bark out a laugh and shake my head. "Nope."

"Well, damn, and I bought dinner and everything."

"I know, it's disappointing." I pat his leg. "There, there."

The drive to my house is quiet, but not uncomfortably so. Lifehouse is playing on the satellite radio, and we roll the windows down to enjoy the warm evening air.

When he pulls into my driveway, I'm almost sad that the drive is over.

"Your house is great," he says, looking at the front of the house. It's an older craftsman-style home, built in the twenties. I replaced the black shutters last year with new ones, and painted it grey with white trim. I have hanging flower baskets on the porch, spilling red, purple, and pink all over the place.

"Thanks. Come eat your cheesecake, and I'll give you a tour."

Once inside, I disarm the alarm, and toss my bag and keys on the table by the front door.

"It's clean." He grins at me. "You were always a clean freak."

"I'm not a clean freak, Camden. I'm barely here. I don't have time to mess it up." I shrug and show him the living room and dining room, along with a half bath on our way back to the kitchen. He sets the dessert bag on the table and pulls out the black dessert boxes, puts them in my fridge, and turns to me.

"Tour first," he says. His arms look amazing tonight. He's

wearing a Henley, and the sleeves are pulled up to his mid-forearms. His biceps and forearm muscles are *crazy*. Not too bulky, but toned, and I want to touch them.

I want to touch *him*. So damn bad. That's why I had to draw the line in the sand right away. No naked shenanigans tonight because this is a first date, and I'm not that kind of girl.

But oh how I wish I was that kind of girl.

"Mia?"

"Yeah?"

"Tour?"

"Right!" I clear my throat and lead him back through the kitchen toward the stairs. "You've pretty much seen most of the first floor. This isn't a huge house, mostly because I don't need a ton of space, and property in this neighborhood is expensive."

"It's a great neighborhood, though."

"I love it here," I reply and climb the stairs ahead of him, knowing full well that he's staring straight at my ass. So, of course I sway my hips just a bit more than really necessary. "Over here—"

Before I can finish my thought, Camden has me shoved against the wall, my hands pinned above my head and his very male, very firm body pressed to mine.

"I noticed the extra sway in your step," he murmurs while teasing my neck with his nose.

"You were supposed to."

He bites me, not gently, and then sweeps his lips over mine.

"That's not the correct way to keep me out of your pants."

"There's a correct way?"

"Yes."

I gasp when he presses his thigh between my legs and rubs against my clit.

"How?"

"I don't know, but that wasn't it."

Just before I drag him into my bedroom, he frees me and shoves his hand through his hair. "Please continue."

No, you *please continue.*

I shake my head and lead him into the guest bedroom.

"This is the guest room."

"And spare closet," he says, nodding at the shoes laid out on the carpet in tidy rows.

"I move them if someone's going to stay here," I reply. "Landon turned Cami's spare bedroom into a huge closet for her. I should do something similar."

"Are you all addicted to clothes?"

"Duh. I'm female. It's in my DNA to love all of the pretty things."

He laughs and follows me through the jack-and-jill bathroom that connects to the other spare bedroom, which I now use as an office. There is only a single desk and chair in here, along with a file cabinet.

"Pretty empty in here."

"Most of my paperwork is done at Seduction, but I use this for a few personal things."

He runs his hand gently down my hair.

"You like to touch me."

"I do," he agrees. His blue eyes are full of lust as he watches me, his hand gliding down my arm now until his fingers link with mine. "I never could keep my hands off you."

I don't know how to respond to that, so I just lead him quickly through my bedroom and bathroom. Actually *lead* isn't the right word. I pull him through as fast as I can.

When we're back in the kitchen, I reach for the fridge, but he stops me.

"Show me your garden."

I spin around to face him. "I said *no* naked time tonight, and we may have a ridiculous amount of chemistry here, but no still means no."

He steps to me and kisses my forehead. "The garden in your backyard, sweetheart."

Oh God, just take me now. How many times can I completely humiliate myself in front of this man?

I spin on my heel and march out the back door, flipping on the backyard floodlight on my way.

"Also, just for future reference, I'll never refer to your pussy as *your garden.* I'm not a ninety-year-old woman."

"There's no need to refer to my pussy at all."

"Oh, trust me, there will be." He's walking through my garden as nonchalantly as possible, as if I didn't just make an ass of myself and we aren't talking about my genitals. "I just use the grown-up words."

"Are you about done?" I ask.

"Nearly." He walks to me and pulls me in for a hug. "Your garden is beautiful, Mia. Both of them."

"Har har."

I can feel the rumble of the laughter in his chest. He's strong and warm, and I could get used to moments like this.

I *can't*. Because this isn't forever. But man, it feels good.

"I'd better go," he whispers.

"You haven't eaten your cheesecake."

"I'll take it with me."

I pull back and look up at him. "What's wrong?"

"If I stay," he begins and drags his fingertips down my cheek. "I won't want to leave *after* the cheesecake. So, it's best if we call it a night now."

I nod and pull away, leading him through the kitchen and out to the front porch. He's holding his cheesecake in one hand, but uses the other to gracefully swoop in and hold me close, kissing me like it's the last time he'll ever see me.

"I'll call you," he says, and then gets in his car and drives away.

"He's gonna call me," I say to no one as I lock my front door. "What is happening?"

Chapter Six

~Camden~

*I*t's on fire," Mia says calmly, as if she's talking about the weather. "What the fuck?"

"You've got the heat too high," I reply as she pulls the pan off of the burner and tosses me a slight glare, making me grin.

"Thanks, captain obvious."

"This is just a rehearsal," Trevor says from his perch off-stage. We're on the set kitchen today, running through two recipes before we start to tape on Monday.

I wrap my arm around Mia's back and press my lips to her ear. "You've got this."

She pushes me away with her hip and shakes her head. "No mushy stuff on set."

I just laugh and return to my own stovetop, stirring the pasta that's just about halfway done.

It's been thirty-six hours since our date. Thirty-six hours since I had my hands on her, my lips on her. She worked herself to the bone yesterday, thanks again to being short-staffed. She wouldn't let me help. It's as if the conversation we had about her control-freak tendencies didn't happen.

I glance over at her and smile. She's stirring her pasta, and her hips are swaying with the movement. She's done that since culinary school. I pull my phone out of my pocket and snap a quick photo just before she tries to reach for a bowl on the top shelf above her workstation.

She can't reach, of course, so I hurry over and grab it for her.

"Trevor, I'm going to need a step stool," she calls out, but I shake my head.

"I've got her back, Trevor."

"This is supposed to be a competition show," she reminds me. "I don't think that includes you *helping* me."

"I'm not an asshole," I remind her as I return to my own chicken, just about done sautéing. "I can help you reach for things, and still kick your ass."

"I'll need that step stool," she says to Trevor, but I shake my head at him. "Stop doing that." She's got her hands propped on her hips now.

"Doing what?"

"Oh my God. Is this how it's going to be? Because I can't work under these conditions."

"Yeah, it must be rough to work with a handsome guy who wants to kiss your ear and help you reach stuff," Riley says from beside her husband. "You might be a bit dramatic."

"He's in *my* kitchen."

"We're on a set," I add.

"Built to look like my kitchen," she counters and I want to boost her up on this countertop and kiss the hell out of her.

"Look out, or you'll burn your chicken again."

"Fucking hell," she mutters and pulls the pan off the heat.

"Maybe less swearing on Monday, when we start taping," Trevor says with a laugh. "Is the stovetop running too hot?"

"No, I'm an idiot," she replies and then clears her throat. "I've got this." She smiles up at the camera that isn't even running yet, and it's amazing to see the transformation from frustrated chef to professional chef. "As you can see, it's easy for the heat to get away from you, especially when you're working with oil. Be sure that it isn't *too* hot. The oil should be ripply, and when you set your chicken in it—with tongs—it sizzles."

The next hour flies by as we finish our dishes. The banter is easy and fun, and I almost forget that this is a competition show.

"Who's going to taste our dishes to decide which is better?" Mia asks after we plate the food and swap plates so we can each have a bite.

"This is good," I say, going in for another bite.

"Of course it is," she replies with a smirk.

"We thought it would be fun to let the crew come on set at the end to taste the dishes and decide on a winner," Trevor replies.

"I like that," Mia says. "It's different."

"Do you have any suggestions for the kitchen?" Trevor asks. "We stocked it with everything on your lists, but if you forgot anything, let us know and we can have it added over the weekend."

"A step stool," Mia says.

"We're good."

"Oh my God," she exclaims in frustration. "You are not the boss of me, Camden Sawyer. If I want a bloody step stool, I'll have the step stool."

"Actually, it's kind of sweet when he reaches for things too high for you," Riley says thoughtfully. "The viewers will eat it up."

"Oh fine," she says with a sigh. "I've already agreed to everything else that I don't want to do, what's one more thing?"

We're all quiet for a few minutes, and then I say to Trevor, "Get the stool."

"It doesn't matter," she says. "Are we done?"

"We are. It went really well, despite the pyrotechnics," Riley says with a smile. "Let's go get a drink. It's happy hour and we should celebrate your first dish cooked in your faux kitchen."

"I'm in," I reply and watch as Mia bites her lip. I can just hear her thoughts. *I should get back to work.*

"Okay," she says at last, surprising us all.

Ten minutes later, we walk into a bar just down the street from the studio. It's busy, loud. But the crowd is a happy one, and thanks to the warm weather, the glass doors are open to the outside.

The hostess leads us to a corner table on the outdoor patio.

"Oh, I'm sorry," the young woman says to Mia. "I'm not sure if you'll fit in that corner chair."

"I'm sitting in the corner," Riley says immediately and takes the seat, leaving the outside seat for Mia, whose cheeks are flushed. She's looking down as she takes her seat and immediately picks up the menu.

The hostess leaves. Riley reaches across the table and squeezes Mia's hand, then turns her attention to her menu.

I'm completely and utterly pissed the fuck off. The hostess just insulted Mia, and Riley covered it up.

But I will *not* have this conversation with Mia right now, in front of her friends and in a public place.

"Today went well," Trevor says. "Mia, you're amazing in front of the camera."

"You're delusional," she says with a grin. I can still see the hurt and embarrassment in her eyes, but she's shaken the hostess off and put on a brave face. "But I'll take all of the compliments."

"You really are great," I reply. "You're great at explaining what you're doing, and why you're doing it. That's the hardest part. I'm so used to cooking, and so much of it is habit, that I really had to practice describing the steps. I can't tell you how many meals I cooked at home, talking out loud when no one was there."

"I talk out loud when no one is there all the time," Riley says with a laugh. "Here comes the waitress. I'm warning you all, I'm ordering all of the happy hour food as well as drinks. I'm starving."

"Oh good," Mia says with a smile. "Me too. Let's order the whole happy hour menu, it's only five things, and share them."

"That's perfect. And we can order more if the portions are small," Riley says with a nod. "Are you guys okay with that?"

"No complaints from me," Trevor says and I nod in agreement. After the waitress leaves with our food and drinks order, Mia lets her hair down from the messy bun and sighs.

"How are you doing?" Riley asks her.

"I'm great."

I take her hand in mine, linking our fingers. She glances over at me, but she doesn't pull her hand away, so I consider that a win.

"You're letting him hold your hand," Riley says. "Is your hand numb, and you just don't feel it, or are you two a thing?"

"Neither. I'm not numb," Mia murmurs. "I let people touch me sometimes."

"Right." Riley nods. "Like when you're unconscious. Or when you go to the doctor and they take your temperature."

"Shut up," Mia says with a laugh. "I let Landon hug me the other night. Not a regular one-armed pat of a hug either. He hugged me against him for like a minute. And I wiped my nose on him."

"Of course you did," Riley says, laughing. She turns to Trevor. "Mia's notorious for not liking to be touched. It's not a trauma thing, she's just not touchy-feely."

I know that Mia has said that she doesn't love to be

touched, but that doesn't describe the Mia I knew years ago at all. She was incredibly affectionate. We snuggled a lot on the couch while watching movies, and she loved to cuddle up to me in bed.

"It's not like I'll stab someone for touching me," she says, interrupting my thoughts. "I just prefer to *not* be. It's not a big deal."

"Except, I don't know if I've ever seen someone hold your hand."

"Shut up, Riley."

"Sorry." But she doesn't look sorry in the least as she grins at Mia. "Not sorry."

Two hours, and three rounds of drinks and food, later, Mia checks the time. "Wow, we've been here for a while."

"Time flies when you're celebrating," Riley says.

I've had my hand on Mia for the past two hours straight. Whether holding her hand or resting on her thigh, I've made sure to touch her. I want her to get used to my touch.

Because I plan on a lot of physical contact later.

"We should go," Trevor says. Mia stands and stretches, reaching high above her. Her shirt rides up, just barely giving me a glimpse of the soft, white skin beneath.

I want to rip that shirt off of her and touch her *everywhere.*

"Are you going back to the restaurant?" I ask her as we push our chairs in and make our way out of the bar.

"Nope." She smiles proudly and tosses me a flirty wink. "I'm going to turn over a new leaf and take the night off."

"Wait. Are you sick?" Riley touches Mia's forehead, but Mia just chuckles.

"I'm not sick. I'm trying to curb my need to control everything there. This is a baby step."

"Atta girl," Riley replies. "Have a good night, you guys."

Trevor and Riley walk away, leaving Mia and me standing in front of the bar. I shove my hands in my pockets and wait for her to say something.

"Do you have plans this evening with your sister?" she asks, staring just past me down the sidewalk, not meeting my gaze.

"Steph and Chip left this morning," I reply. "I don't have any plans."

She nods and shuffles her feet. "Well, I don't know if you've heard, but I'm curbing my control-freak tendencies this evening."

"I did hear something about that," I say and step toward her. "You should probably be supervised. Just to make sure that you don't give in and rush back to your kitchen."

She nods slowly. "That would probably be a good idea. I mean, I can't be expected to be reformed in a day. That's just ridiculous."

"What would you like to do, Mia?"

She smiles up at me and reaches for my hand. "I'd like to bake brownies and drink decaf coffee on my back porch."

Before or after I make you forget your name?

"Let's do it."

I follow her to her house and park behind her in the

driveway. She waits for me as I climb out of my car and join her on the porch.

"Are we baking brownies from scratch?" I ask as she unlocks her door and I follow her inside.

"No, that takes too long," she replies. "I have a good box mix. I'll add a few extra things to it."

"Brownies take an hour to bake," I remind her.

"Yep."

"What are we going to do for an hour?"

"Get naked," she replies with a shrug. "And then we will have fresh brownies. I mean, is there a better post-coital snack than brownies?"

I stop and stare at her, watching as she grins and pulls the ingredients for the chocolate dessert out of cupboards and the fridge. I pull my phone out of my pocket and snap a picture of her as she stirs the batter. When she glances at me, I snap another one, happy to capture the bright smile she gives me.

"Are you taking photos of me?"

"I want visual proof that you actually bake."

She laughs and pours the batter into a pan. "I told you, I can bake with the best of them. I do all of the baking at Seduction."

"I'm impressed," I reply after she shuts the oven door and sets the timer.

One hour.

Her eyes look less certain now that the task of getting the brownies ready to bake is over, and I'm slowly advancing on her here in her kitchen.

She's not moving away.

"Mia."

She looks up, and when I glide my hands down her sides and around to her ass, then lift her onto the countertop, she simply bites her lip and watches me with wide, curious blue eyes.

"Are you sure you want this?" I whisper. I've caged her in, my hands are flat on the countertop next to her hips. Her legs are spread, and I'm pressed against her. I drag my nose down hers and then nibble lightly on her lips. "Mia."

"Hmm."

"I asked a question."

"I invited you here."

"That wasn't the question," I reply and kiss her chin and up her jawline to her ear. "I want you to tell me, with words, that you want me, Mia. I want to strip you out of these clothes and touch every inch of this amazing body."

She bites her lip again and I see a brief moment of uncertainty pass through her eyes.

"You have to talk to me, baby."

"I don't really look like I did ten years ago."

"None of us do."

She shakes her head and leans back so she can look me in the eyes. "I've gained weight, Camden, and it makes me uncomfortable."

"I have always loved every curve on your body. I hate that you have insecurities, but I'm telling you right now, you don't have to feel uncomfortable with me. We can take this as slow or as fast as you want. We don't even have to get all the way naked, but I admit, that would make me pout."

She grins slowly. "I wouldn't want you to pout."

"No, it's not attractive at all. But all kidding aside, tonight is all about you. I'm here because you invited me, and because I want to spend the evening with you. I want you, Mia. I won't lie and say I don't. But I'm a patient man."

"That's new," she says with a raised eyebrow. She leans forward and presses a kiss over my sternum, through my shirt. "You may be patient. But I'm not."

"No?"

"No."

Her hair is down. It's longer than I've ever seen on her, and it's absolutely sexy as hell. Her neck is smooth, the skin there so fucking soft. She gathers my shirt in her fists and pulls up so she can glide her hands on my bare skin.

"If you keep doing that, the patience will fly out of the window."

She smiles and tilts her head to the side, giving me all the invitation I need. I press the tip of my tongue against the softest skin right below her ear and drag it down to her collarbone. I kiss over to the other side and back up to the other ear, soaking her in.

Her breathing has sped up, matching my own. She pulls back and peels her top over her head, tossing it on the floor. I reach over my shoulder and pull my shirt off as well.

"Do men take a class on how to take off their shirt in the sexiest way possible?"

"It's in our DNA," I reply.

"It's impressive," she says before leaning in and kissing

my chest. She bites me gently on the collarbone, and then my neck.

"I forgot what a biter you are," I murmur. I make quick work of getting her out of her bra, toss it aside, and cup her breasts in my palms, worrying the already hard nipples between my thumbs and forefingers. "Your breasts are fantastic."

She tips her head back with a sigh as I suck on one, then the other. Her body is a bit softer than before. Rounder.

I can't get enough of it.

She's reaching for my pants, and all I can think about is tasting her.

"Living room," I mutter and carry her to the sectional. I set her down and we strip out of our clothes, throwing them aside, unable to keep our hands off each other. I'm cupping her face and kissing the fuck out of her. Her hands are traveling down my sides, and just before she grips my cock in her sexy little hand, I pull back.

"If you touch me, I'll have to fuck you now and it'll be over." I swallow hard when determination darkens her blue eyes. "I'm serious, Mia, we have an hour."

"Probably closer to forty-five minutes now," she says breathlessly.

"I'm not going to rush this." I kiss her lips gently, and guide her down to the couch. "I want to explore you a bit."

She bites her lip.

She's such a fucking biter, it's going to be the death of me.

"You're so beautiful," I mutter and let my fingertips explore her chest, her arms, over the slight swell of her belly and her thighs. "Lie down."

She complies, and I silently thank her for buying this big sofa, big enough for her to lie down and for me to lie on my stomach, her legs over my shoulders.

I'm not there yet, but I will be very soon.

"I haven't had a shower since this morning," she informs me, already guessing what I have planned.

"I give zero fucks about that." I drag my knuckles over her nipples, making them pucker again; and kiss her belly, right below her navel. She sighs in pleasure when I tickle that spot with my nose. My hands are travelling all over her now, slowly, softly. Her eyelids are heavy as she watches me. "Close your eyes, Mia. And hold on to the cushion over your head."

Her eyes flash in excitement before she complies. Her skin is white and soft. Tender. Responsive.

I kiss just above her pubis. She's not waxed, but she's trimmed, and I can't help but wonder if she did that for me.

Her legs scissor as my fingertips gently brush over her armpits, and down her sides, setting goosebumps on fire over her body.

"If you want me to stop, you just say the word. Do you understand?"

"For the love of God, please don't stop."

I grin and lick the inside of her right thigh, then the left one. Once I'm settled with her legs over my shoulders, I press my thumb against her clit and suck the lips of her pussy into my mouth, making pulsing motions. Her entire body tenses and then releases as she writhes in pleasure.

"You're so sweet." I lick one lip, then the other, before moving up to pull her clit into my mouth.

"Jesus, Camden." Her hips buck. I push my hands under her ass and hold her up, giving me better access to her entire core.

"Yes?"

"I can't." Her head thrashes back and forth as I lick, and suck, and nibble every spot of skin. When I press my tongue to her clit and rub up and down quickly, she comes apart spectacularly, crying out, her body flushing and shivering.

I need to be inside of her. Right now.

Chapter Seven

~Mia~

He's trying to fucking kill me. Dead. Deader than dead. My body is humming from the intense orgasm he just gave me, and the next thing I know he turns me, as if I weigh nothing, on the couch so my ass is at the edge of the cushion. He reaches for his jeans, protecting us both, and returns his attention to me.

His body is ridiculous. Bronze, as if God made him look permanently tanned. His muscles are toned, his stomach flat. A light, fine spattering of hair covers his chest and thins as it flows south to his cock.

And the cock is something to write home about.

Not that I will.

"In me," I instruct him, looking down.

"Look at me."

My eyes fly to his in a heartbeat. They're deep blue, full

of lust, and are pinned to mine as he takes his cock in his fist and drags the tip through my wet folds, over my clit, and makes me fling my head back.

"My God."

"Look at me," he says again. I comply, and he slowly slides inside me. When he's fully buried to the hilt, he bends over and kisses me sweetly. He links he fingers with mine, and kisses the back of my hand. "You're so fucking sweet."

I bite my lip and flex around him, silently begging him to fucking *move*.

"Mia."

"Love it when you say my name."

He grins and pulls out halfway, then moves back in. "Do you?"

"Yeah."

"What else do you like?"

"The list is long."

His lips wrap around a nipple, making me arch my back and shove my fingers into the hair at the back of his head. "That. I like that."

With a growl, he pulls me off the couch and onto the white, shag rug I bought two weeks ago. It's soft against my back. He's kneeling and my back is still arched, my hips up to meet his. He's got a death grip on my hips, pushing and pulling as he slowly begins to work his way in and out of me.

I can't even stand how good it feels. Has it ever felt like this? I don't think so. I don't even know if it's legal in the state of Oregon to feel like this.

It shouldn't be.

His palm slides from my stomach to my throat in one long, fluid motion and then back down again. He plants the pad of his thumb against my clit, and just like that I start to see stars.

"Camden."

"Yes, baby." He's pulsing inside me, tiny movements that hit that damn spot over and over again, and I'm about to come harder than ever. "That's it."

I cover my face with my hands and cry out as the orgasm moves through me, making every nerve ending in my body tingle spectacularly.

He lowers my ass to the ground and covers me now, buries his face in my neck and groans with his own release. I'm happy to lie here for a long moment, cradling him against me, soaking in the weight of him, touching his body during one of his most vulnerable moments.

It's just bliss. It was always bliss when it came to sex with Camden. But this time is just a little bit . . . *different.* Not bad. Not bad at all. My body feels alive. Along with the bliss, there's a *longing* . . . a sweetness that wasn't there when we were younger.

It's better than before, and I didn't think that was possible.

"What are you thinking?" he asks against my ear, just as the oven timer dings.

"That the brownies are done."

"That's a lie," he says and kisses my cheek, then my lips. He's propped on his elbows, looking down at me.

"They're going to burn."

"Then you'd better answer me quickly."

I sigh and drag my fingertips down his face. "I was thinking that slow sex feels pretty damn good."

He eyes me for a moment, then smiles. "Taking it fast, especially this time, wasn't an option, Mia. And for the record—I'm going to say right here and now, so there is no misunderstanding—this wasn't just about a quick fuck."

"That's not romantic," I mutter.

"Exactly. I don't know what will happen, but this *is* exclusive. I don't want there to be any confusion."

Like before, when I was dumb.

I nod thoughtfully. "Good to know."

He winks and rolls away. I reach for my shirt and throw it over my head as I race to the kitchen and take the brownies out of the oven.

"The edges are just a tiny bit overdone. They'll be chewy."

"Excellent. I like them that way." I look back at him and almost swallow my tongue. He pulled his jeans on, but didn't button them, and he's not wearing a shirt.

"Do you have a license for that?"

"For what?"

"For the way you look. It's ridiculous."

He laughs and tugs his black T-shirt over his head, making me purse my lips in a pout. "You didn't have to put that back on."

"I don't mind being your eye candy," he says, kissing me.

"Well, that's good. Because you are whether you like it or not. It just *is*."

"Do you have ice cream to go with the brownies?" He

walks over to the freezer and opens it, surveying the contents.

"I'm no amateur," I reply with a laugh. "You serve dessert while I go clean up a bit."

He grabs my ass and kisses my neck. "You don't have to wear pants."

"I do. I do have to wear pants."

Now he pouts, and I pat his cheek playfully. "You can take them back off later."

"Deal."

I can hear him rustling through my kitchen, looking for serving utensils and plates, as I clean up and throw on clean clothes. I forgo the underwear, just because I'm feeling sassy.

When I rejoin him, he's plated the brownies with ice cream, and found a sprig of mint to put on the top of each one.

"Fancy."

He turns and smiles at me. "Why shouldn't I make it fancy for you? I'm trying to impress you."

"It might be working," I reply with a shrug and take my plate from him, leading him onto my front porch.

"This space is great," he says, settling in next to me.

"I wanted a screened-in porch," I say, and take a bite of the melty ice cream and hot brownie. "Dear God, that's good."

"Make noises like that, Mia, and I'll take you right here on the porch where everyone can hear you."

"No, you won't." I lean against him and chew thoughtfully. "I wanted the porch to be screened in because I like to eat out here, but I don't like bugs."

"Makes sense."

"Everyone made fun of me."

"I don't like to have bugs around while I eat either. I don't see why they'd make fun of you for it."

"Well, by everyone I mean Landon, and he pretty much makes fun of me for everything."

Camden nods and finishes his treat, sets the plate to the side, and wraps his arms around me while I continue to eat. "I make fun of my sister for just about everything too. It's what we do."

"I get it."

"Your brownies are delicious."

"Yeah, this is turning out to be a religious experience."

He chuckles and kisses my temple. "You make me laugh."

I finish my brownie and set the plate next to Camden's, then sit quietly in his arms for a long moment, just enjoying the evening with him. Once in a while a car will drive by, interrupting the quiet, and then it settles around us again.

"Are you sleepy?" he asks.

"I'm getting there. Let's sit out here for a while."

"I'd like to stay."

It's not a question. He's not asking if he *can*. And I definitely don't want him to leave.

"You should stay."

He nods and we sit like this for a long time, watching the neighborhood, enjoying each other. The silence isn't uncomfortable. In fact, I don't remember the last time I felt this content.

This safe.

My eyes are heavy, so I let them close and enjoy the sounds around me. The frogs and Camden's even breathing.

"Mia."

"Hmm."

"You're sleeping, sweetheart."

"I'm just resting my eyes."

"Let's go to bed."

I sit up, stretch, and reach for the plates. "Maybe I am tired."

"I know I am. You wore me out."

"Sure I did." I laugh and lock the door, turn off the lights, and set the plates in the kitchen sink. Camden checks the lock on the back door and reaches out for my hand.

"Come on, you can wear me out some more."

IT'S NOT SUNDAY, which sucks ass. It means that I can't lie in bed and be lazy until it's time to go have brunch with the girls. It also means that it's Saturday, and it's going to be so fucking busy at work that I'll drop back into bed tonight as a zombie. My feet will be numb. My hair will smell. I'll be alone.

Wait.

I may *not* be alone.

In fact, if memory serves, I'm not alone right now.

Without opening my eyes, I reach out and feel around in my king-sized bed, but I don't encounter any warm, manly flesh. Just cool sheets.

I frown and open one bleary eye, looking around in confusion. Camden spent the night last night. If he sneaked out of here and left me a cliché note on the pillow, I'll hunt him down and throat punch him.

I might be a tiny bit grouchy in the morning. But damn it, I'm too old to hook up with men who sneak out before morning.

"She's awake."

Without sitting up, I turn my head and find Camden standing in the doorway of my bedroom, holding a tray with steaming food on it.

"I have to work this morning," I remind him, but he just smirks and carries the tray to my bed, sets it down at the end of the bed and leans over to kiss me.

I haven't brushed my teeth, so I'm mildly horrified as he pulls away.

"I made breakfast. You didn't have much in the fridge, so you're stuck with a bacon and cheese omelet. No side."

"That's more than I usually eat." I sit up, wrap the sheet around me and lean against the headboard.

Camden snaps a picture of me on his phone.

"Are you an amateur photographer?"

I reach for the coffee first and take a sip.

"I like the way you look," he replies as he strips out of his boxers and joins me in bed. He reaches for the food, grabs one of the two forks, and takes a bite of the omelet.

"I thought you said that was for me?"

"It's for both of us. You only had enough for one."

Reaching for my fork, I lean in and kiss his shoulder as I load up the eggy, cheesy goodness. "Thanks for doing this."

"You're welcome. I didn't want to wake you up."

"I need to get up anyway. I should get to Seduction early to start prepping for today. Saturday is our busiest day of the week as it is, but Jake is playing tonight, so we will be packed."

"Jake Knox," he says with a nod. "I haven't met him yet."

"Come by this evening and you will."

He takes one more bite and sets his fork down, leaving the last bite for me. "I'd like to come help today, Mia."

"It's not—"

"My job, I know, but damn it, you need the help. I'll be bored, wandering around the city of Portland aimlessly and alone, while you get to have fun in the kitchen all day. It's not fair." He sighs deeply, as if the weight of the world is on his shoulders, and I can't help but smile at him.

"You're a nice guy."

"Now you're just being mean. The hot girl *never* wants the nice guy."

"I don't know what the hot girl wants, but *I* like the nice guy."

"You're the hot girl." He kisses my cheek. "I'm going to take a selfie."

I frown. "I look horrible."

"No, you don't." He raises the camera, and rather than smile at the lens, I rest my forehead on his jaw. "That's okay, this is a cute picture."

He shows it to me, and I have to agree. He's smiling big, bare chested, his dark blond hair a mess. My eyes are closed, and it looks like a sweet, intimate moment between the two of us.

"Will you send it to me?"

"I'll post it on social media, too."

I pull back in surprise. "No, you won't."

"Okay, I won't." He grins and texts the picture to me. "Tell me I won't be alone and sad today while you have fun at work."

"We can't have that." I wipe my lips on the napkin and toss it on the tray. "You can come in."

"Great."

"I have to take a quick shower so I can get ready for work."

"Even better."

"Do *not* interrupt me in the shower. I had time for sex *or* breakfast. You made your choice."

"Bullshit," he calls after me.

The hot water feels so good on my sore body. I'm deliciously sore, muscles that I didn't know I had are weeping. I guess that's what happens when you have sex several times through the night after a long dry spell.

Just as I'm finishing up, the glass door of my walk-in shower opens and in walks a very naked, very aroused Camden.

"Hi," he says with a smile. "I came to wash your back."

"I was just about to get out."

"Good. I didn't really want to wash your back." He pins me against the wall of the shower, and kisses me, holding my hands above my head with one hand and letting his other roam all over my slick body. "You're fucking sexy in the morning."

"Camden."

"Yes."

"I hate to burst this lusty bubble, but water sex isn't really comfortable for me."

He leans back and looks down at me with a frown. "In what way?"

Well this isn't uncomfortable at all.

"I'm just going to say it."

"We're both adults here."

"For a lot of women, me included, when you have sex in the water, it washes away the natural lubrication and it hurts *so fucking bad.*"

"I'm a thirty-two-year-old man, and I've never heard this before."

"Probably because no one wanted to say anything. You don't want to ruin the moment and all that. But I'm already a little sore from last night, and if we do this *here,* I will be in agony, and I have to be on my feet all day."

"No problem."

He picks me up and spins around, pinning me against the opposite wall. I can feel the hot water on my legs and feet, but it's nowhere near my vagina.

"Better?"

"Oh yeah."

He grins and kisses me softly, slowly as he slides inside me, also at a happily lazy pace. It seems that when it comes to sex, Camden doesn't do anything quickly.

Which, in this moment, works well for me. My tired, oversexed muscles have the chance to adjust to him again before he starts to move. His thrusts are shallow, so he stays buried deep inside me.

It's fucking amazing.

"Mia," he murmurs against my neck.

"Yes."

"I want to stay here with you, all day, and do this. Relearn you. Feed you. Laugh with you. Fuck you."

I bite his shoulder as his pubis presses on my clit and moan. My fingernails are digging into his back.

"I can't hold on."

"Don't." He bites my neck, just the way I like it, and that's all it takes to send me over the edge, riding the wave of ecstasy that washes over me.

He sets me gently on my feet and I immediately kneel. I wash off his cock and then suck him, working him over with both hands and my mouth. His moans and gasps of delight fuel my hunger to please him, to make him as crazy as he makes me.

He calls out my name and comes, making a mess of me, and I don't care. He's shivering and weak, and I feel like the most powerful woman in the world as I stand and wash off, then leave him to clean up in the shower while I towel off.

"Was that okay?" he asks, still breathing hard.

"Oh yeah. I think you've figured out the water sex hack."

He nods. "Good. Because we'll be doing that again."

I want to stay here with you, all day, and do this. Relearn you. Feed you. Laugh with you. Fuck you.

His words are on a constant loop in my head. For the first time that I can remember, I *want* to stay home. I want to blow off work and stay home with him, doing all of the things he described. I wish I had another chef on staff that I trusted to take care of things without me.

I've never given this a thought before, but it's not a bad one. He's right, I need people in my kitchen that I trust. What if I was sick? Or in an accident? The kitchen has to be able to function without me.

I'll talk with Cami later about the budget and how much we can afford.

"You okay?" he asks as he joins me in my bedroom. He's just toweled off. He kisses me on the shoulder.

"Yeah."

"You're just standing here," he says with a smile and reaches for his clothes. "Are you sure?"

"I'm great." I smile, excited that he's going to come help today. "Are you sure you want to give up your Saturday to work at the restaurant?"

"I'm not giving up anything, baby." He glances around to make sure he has everything. "But I'm going to have to meet you there. I'll need to swing by my place and change my clothes."

"No problem."

"Drive safely," he says as he walks out of the room. "I'll see you in a bit. I'll bring Starbucks."

"Oh Lord," I mutter after I hear the front door close. "I could fall in love with him. Again."

Chapter Eight

~Camden~

"Tonight's show was fantastic, as always," Addie says as she kisses her husband, Jake. It's after closing time, and we're gathered in the bar, unwinding before we all head home.

"You might be biased," Jake says with a grin.

"Well, I'm not biased," I reply. "It was pretty great."

"Thank you," he says with a nod. "It's always fun to play here. That's how Addie and I met, you know."

"No, I didn't know."

"We put out an ad for a weekend musician," Addie says, "and Jake came in to apply for it."

"Were ticket sales down?" I ask.

"I hadn't performed in a long time," he says. "And I missed it. But I don't ever want to go back to touring. The band isn't getting back together. I'm happy producing music, but I liked the idea of getting on a small stage with my guitar. And the rest is history."

"He's a busy man, so he only performs once a month now," Addie adds. "We have a little girl, and he has a business to run."

"How did you and Mia meet?" Jake asks.

"In culinary school," Mia says as she methodically takes her hair down, as is her habit most nights after work. Kat passes us both a glass of wine from behind the bar.

"I don't think I've heard this story," Kat says. "Spill it."

"Don't you have a husband to go home to?" Mia asks with a scowl.

"He'll still be there after you tell me the story," Kat replies with a grin.

"I actually like our story," I say and look to Mia. She nods, and I launch into it. "So, Mia and I went to culinary school together up near Seattle. That's where I'm originally from. Mia and I were assigned to be lab partners, which worked for me. I mean, look at her."

"Don't look at me. I'm a mess."

"You're beautiful," I reply. "Even when you're a mess." Kat and Addie exchange a glance, but I keep talking. "Anyway, it didn't hurt my feelings at all to work with Mia. She was funny and smart, and she had a great work ethic even then."

"I am pretty awesome." Mia smirks and sips her wine.

"She would get these ideas, and run with them. And I would just step back and follow her lead."

"What does *that* mean?" Mia's scowling at me.

"Well, you're bossy. You have a successful restaurant for

a reason, Mia. Even if the rest of the place is amazing, people won't come back if the chef sucks. You're not exactly warm and fuzzy, but you control everything around you."

"I'm not *warm and fuzzy* enough for you?" she asks—her voice deadly calm—and I know that I've just royally fucked things up, but I have no idea how.

"It's not an insult, Mia. You know that I loved working with you in school."

"Even though I was a bitch," she says, nodding.

"Whoa. I didn't call you a bitch."

"You know, you weren't complaining about my level of warm and fuzzy last night when you fucked me all night."

"Enough." My voice is stern, and I'm disappointed in her. "We'll talk about this in private."

"No need." She shakes her head and chugs the last of her wine before slamming the glass down so hard that the stem breaks. "There's no need to be around me if you think I'm a bitch. I mean, no one wants to be around someone who's not warm and fuzzy."

She stands and marches out of the bar and I'm blinking in confusion.

"What the fuck just happened?" I ask.

"It's not your fault," Addie says. "Sometimes Mia gets a little touchy about her stern work ethic. People have quit and marched out, calling her a cunt, and a bitch, and every other name in the book on their way out the door. They think she's too tough on her staff, but really she just wants them to *want* to do well. To be competent at their job."

"She really just needs a whole day off once in a while,"

Kat says. "Of all of us, I'd say the transition has been the hardest for her. But she won't talk about it with us."

"I see." I stand and nod at the others before I follow the way Mia went. I find her standing near the hostess stand, her head bowed. "Mia."

She sniffles and quickly wipes her cheeks dry. "What?"

"I didn't mean to make you cry."

God, please don't cry. That's the worst thing that a woman can do to a man. We just aren't equipped to deal with tears.

"I'm not crying," she says, but another tear slips out of the corner of her eye and onto her cheek. "Damn it."

"I wasn't insulting you, sweetheart. Your work ethic is amazing. It's one of the things that I admire the most about you. You kick my ass, that's for sure."

"I'm not insulted."

"Come here."

She pauses and bites her lip, and then her face crumples in tears and she throws herself into my arms, hugging me tightly around the middle. Her face is buried in my chest as she cries.

"Shh." I rub my hand in circles around her back. "Sweetheart, it's okay."

"I don't know what's wrong with me."

"Talk to me."

"I'm not mean. I'm not cold or heartless."

"No, you're absolutely *not* those things."

"I mean, I expect a certain level of professionalism. I always have. The kitchen should be clean and organized.

Everyone needs to be mindful of what they're doing. Pay fucking attention."

"Otherwise people get hurt," I add, agreeing wholeheartedly with her.

"Yes!" She nods. "Exactly. I don't know what's wrong with people, but let me just say, very few people share our views on that. And when it happens in *my* kitchen, they get thrown out on their ass."

"As it should be."

"But I've been called so many hateful, hurtful, horrible things, Camden. All my life, really, but especially since I've been running this business. And I don't get it. Why would anyone call me a cock-sucking cunt on their way out of my kitchen? They'll never get a letter of recommendation from me for that. And the restaurant community is small. We talk. It's career suicide to abuse a master chef that way."

"Not to mention, it just makes them an asshole," I say, so angry that I want to have just five minutes alone with any asshole who ever spoke to her this way. "You don't deserve that, Mia. Ever."

"No, I don't. But it happens more than you think. So after the last one quit in the middle of his shift and told me that I could bend over and take his dick up my ass before he'd ever follow another order from me again, I decided to not fill the position. I'd rather work myself, eighty hours a week, than put up with that."

"Honestly, I'd like a list of anyone who's treated you like that."

She sighs and wipes her cheeks. "And I can be warm and fuzzy. It just doesn't belong in the kitchen."

"Maybe if we're alone in the kitchen you can be warm and fuzzy," I suggest and the knot in my stomach loosens when I feel her chuckle against me.

"Maybe."

"Are you okay?"

She takes a deep breath. "Yeah. It's been a stressful week, and Mother Nature always makes me mean to people I like." She whispers *a lot* under her breath.

"You mean, you have *female* things happening."

"Yeah. It ruins everything."

I hug her tightly and then pull back and smile down at her. "Let's go to my place. It's not far from here. I'll take care of you."

She blinks rapidly. "Camden, I don't know if you're aware what Mother Nature means, but all you have to do is feed me and tell me I'm pretty."

"I know what it means. We'll save earth-shattering sex for another day. Trust me."

She wipes the last of her tears away. "I do. Let's go."

"YOU MADE ME cupcakes," she says, her eyes still heavy with sleep. She sits up and stares in wonder as I slip a plate of three cupcakes on her lap. "And let me nap."

I grin and watch as she takes a big bite of the chocolate goodness, then sighs in happiness.

"Oh, these are good."

"You're pretty," I reply and tuck a strand of her hair behind her ear.

"You're good at following directions," she says and kisses my hand. "Food and compliments are really all I need on a day like today."

"I'm happy to help. You didn't sleep well last night."

She tossed and turned, and when she finally did sleep, it was fitful.

"Neither did you. I think I kicked you at one point."

"Nowhere important." I watch her take another bite of her cake. "Are you okay?"

"Yeah, I'm fine." She shrugs one shoulder and then looks me in the eyes. "I really am okay. I have no complaints at all."

"But?"

"But this is all a surprise."

"The cupcakes?"

She laughs and shakes her head no. "You. This. I wasn't expecting it."

"What were you expecting?"

"Honestly?"

"Always."

"Resentment, anger, attitude. All of those would have been normal, given our past. I didn't expect you to want to start something new."

"I felt all of those things for a while," I admit, thinking back on those days just after I found her gone. How angry I was. How I couldn't stand to live in that apartment after she moved out and I moved back in with Steph for a while. "But it's been a long time, and we've talked a lot of it out. We're not the same people we were, and I have to tell you, relearning who you are has been pretty great."

"Were there a lot of women? After me?" Her cheeks flush in embarrassment, but she keeps her chin high. "Maybe I'm hormonal, but I'm curious."

"There have been some," I admit and shrug one shoulder, watching as she peels the paper off a cupcake. "Nothing serious. Maybe I compared them to you."

"That's not healthy."

"I don't think I did it consciously, but no one compared to you, Mia."

"I think you're pretty great," she says, and leans in to kiss me. "I'm glad you're here, and that Riley stood her ground. I wasn't very excited when they told me who the celebrity chef was that they wanted me to work with."

"I'm sure."

"Mostly, I'd put it all squarely in the past, and I had never mentioned you to any of the girls or my family. Like I said before, I was embarrassed, and I'd moved on. But I think I still carried a lot of shame and anxiety over the way I handled things, and I feel lighter now."

"Me too," I reply. "Have you filled them all in now?"

"No." She finishes her second cupcake and sighs. "Landon and Cami know it all because I just had to talk to someone about it. The others know bits and pieces. We'll probably have a girls night soon. I'll drink too much and spill everything, then throw up and all will be right with the world again."

"Really. Is that what women do?"

"That's what these women do."

"Good to know." I laugh and kiss her forehead. "What would you like to do with the rest of your Sunday?"

"What time is it?"

"Just past one. You napped for a while."

"Shit," she mutters and reaches for her phone. "I have to do dinner with my parents tonight. We do it one Sunday every month, and it's today."

I quickly rethink my plans for an evening in with lasagna and movies. "When do you have to leave?"

"Around three. Mom and Dad like to eat early. I think it's a law that older people have to eat dinner before five. Oh, and you're coming with me."

"I am? Why?"

Her head jerks up. "You don't want to go?"

"I didn't say that."

"Well, Landon and Cami won't be there today, so I thought it would be a quiet way for you to meet them. But maybe I'm being dumb. You don't have to go at all. In fact, forget I said anything."

I cover her mouth with mine, effectively shutting her up.

"I will go with you."

"Is it weird?"

"No. I told you, this isn't just about sex. I'd like to meet your parents."

"Okay." She nods and texts her mother. "I'm letting her know that I'm bringing a man. You do know that because they're old fashioned, and because they're my parents, my mother will have the wedding planned before we leave."

"That's convenient." I bark out a laugh when she stares at me in horror. "It'll be fun. I'm quite charming when I meet new people."

"This might just make you run back to L.A."

"I doubt it." I kiss her again and she wiggles away, stands, and finger-combs her hair.

"I have to get ready."

"You look fine to me."

"I have to go home and change my clothes."

"Let's go. We'll just take one car."

"You're a bit bossy."

"Hello, pot."

She laughs and accepts my hand, letting me lead her out to my car. "Get used to it."

"So, where are you from, Camden?" Mia's mom asks. The four of us are seated around the table in Mia's parents' home. They're polite, and I can tell by the glint in their eyes that they're *very* interested in what my intentions are with their daughter.

Not that I can tell them that. I haven't even told *Mia* that.

"Kirkland, just outside of Seattle."

"Nice area," her father says.

We've spent the past hour talking about television, being a chef, and how pretty Mia was as a baby. The latter much to Mia's dismay.

"What Mia needs is a nice man to settle down with," Mrs. Palazzo says, making Mia's eyes go wider than I've ever seen them.

"Mother!"

"It's the truth," her dad says. "You should get married and have babies. You're not getting any younger, and you have the hips for it. You would give us plenty of grandchildren."

"I sure wish the floor would open up and swallow me now," Mia says, pinching the bridge of her nose. I can't help it. All I can do is sit back in my seat and laugh.

"Well, I mean, does Mia come with a dowry?" I ask, unable to keep from smiling when Mia glares daggers at me. Her father's eyes narrow, as if he's considering it.

"I'm sure we could come up with a mutually beneficial agreement."

"Mom."

"He's kidding," her mother says, but Mia shakes her head no.

"He's not kidding. Make it stop."

"We are certainly not arranging for Mia to have a dowry," she says sternly.

"I'm completely kidding," I add, holding my hands up in surrender. "Mia doesn't need a dowry."

Her father almost pouts as he takes a bite of his garlic bread.

"I see where Mia gets her talent for cooking. This is delicious."

"I like him," Mrs. Palazzo says with a nod. "Mia, come help me with dessert."

"If you're not here when I get back, I totally understand," Mia says. "I had no idea that my parents would *actually* try to talk you into marrying me."

"I'm fine," I reply honestly. "Go get us dessert."

She glares at her father. "Be nice."

When Mia and her mother are in the kitchen, Mr. Palazzo smiles at me with a shrug. "It's fun to rile her up."

"I couldn't agree more."

"Of course her mother and I want her to find a special man. We want many grandchildren. But the most important thing is that Mia finds someone worthy of her."

"I don't know if that man exists," I reply. "She's a special woman."

"Yes. She is. Recognizing that is the most important first step. I can see that you're smitten with my girl."

"She's a special woman," I repeat just as his telephone rings.

"Excuse me."

He walks out of the room, and I can hear Mia and her mother talking in the kitchen.

"I made you a sugar-free option." It's her mother's voice.

"Why would you do that?"

"In case you're giving up sugar."

"I never said I was giving up sugar."

There's a sigh.

"Also, why in the name of all that's holy would Dad say that I have birthing hips?"

I grin, not at all ashamed that I'm listening in.

"Maybe because you do," her mother says. "It's okay, Mia. Having children is nothing to be ashamed of."

"Oh Lord," Mia mutters. "I don't think Camden cares that I have hips."

Doesn't give even one fuck.

"Of course not," her mother says. "He's clearly very taken with you."

"And he's not Italian," Mia says.

"Sorry, I had to take that," her father says as he joins me. A moment later, the ladies come out with a delicious-looking tiramisu.

The rest of the dinner is much of the same conversation, and once the dishes are finished, Mia takes my hand and announces that we need to leave.

"Thank you for coming," her mother says as she gives us each a kiss on the cheek. "I hope we get to see you again, Camden."

Mia rushes me out of the house and down to my car, and after we've pulled away from the curb, she lets out a long, painful sigh.

"That didn't go well," she says.

"Why not?"

"I mean, I knew that they'd drop hints about marriage. I'm their only daughter and they're convinced that my biological clock is ticking. I get that. But they acted as if I've never introduced them to a man before. It's like, they're *shocked* that I snagged a date, so they're going to drill it home that they want me married. STAT."

"And that's just insulting. This is the twenty-first century."

"They love you," I reply and take her hand in mine, kissing her knuckles. "They were pretty obvious, but it wasn't in a malicious way. They want you to be happy."

"I *am* happy."

"Good. That's all they need."

"We clearly weren't at the same dinner. I'm sorry that it was so embarrassing. I shouldn't have invited you."

"Look at me." She complies. "Do I look angry or embarrassed?"

"No. Why is that?"

"Because I'm neither of those things. They are loving parents. Trust me, just feel happy that you have parents to fuss over you."

"I'm sorry," she says immediately. "I don't mean to sound ungrateful. It just made me incredibly uncomfortable."

"I can see that. But I'm fine, so let it roll off your back. It's not a big deal."

She nods and looks out the passenger window.

"I think I'll go home tonight," she says softly.

"We can stay at your place."

"Maybe I'll go alone."

I glance at her. "Why?"

"We start filming tomorrow, and I don't feel as good as I could. It might just be better if we spend tonight apart and regroup."

"Is that what you want to do?"

She swallows hard and then nods, putting on a brave smile. "Yeah."

"Well, I don't." I pull up to my rental house and turn to face her. "I don't know where this is coming from. I suspect you're still feeling embarrassed, and I'm going to say this one last time. Your parents are fine. I thought it was funny. I'm not here because they made me feel sorry for you."

She winces.

"I'm here because I think you're badass and I like who I am when I'm with you. So if you want to stay at your place tonight, that's fine. But you won't be staying alone."

She's quiet for a moment and then she licks her lips and meets my gaze. "Pack a bag."

Chapter Nine

~Mia~

There's a woman with a makeup brush standing to my left. "I don't need any more makeup."

"You do," she insists. "Just some powder so the lights don't make you shiny."

I roll my eyes and stand still as she dusts my face for the fourth time in an hour.

"Are we ready?" Trevor asks us.

"Ready." I nod and take a deep breath. I don't love being in front of the camera, but I'm getting better at it.

Camden leans in and whispers in my ear, "You look so fucking sexy. You've got this."

I glance up at him, smirk, and bump him with my hip, making him chuckle and walk back to his workstation.

"Action."

"Don't forget," I begin and check the oil on the stove-top. "You don't want the oil to be too hot. It *will* catch on fire."

"Just like it did during rehearsal," Camden adds with a wink.

"Yeah, Camden set the place on fire." I laugh and gently set my chicken in the hot oil.

"It wasn't me," he says, shaking his head, also placing his chicken in his own skillet.

I walk over to pull some oregano out of the cupboard, but it's too high for me. As always. Trevor had a step stool brought in, but I'm feeling particularly flirty today, so I set it aside and look at Camden.

"I could use some help."

"Of course." He reaches up for the herb and hands it to me. "Need anything else?"

"Not right now."

He nods and returns to his skillet and I wink at the cam-era. "Here's a good rule to have in your kitchen: Never use a step stool when there's a perfectly capable, tall man in the kitchen with you."

"I see. You're just using me." Camden laughs and points out his technique for deciding when the chicken is done to the camera.

We spend the next thirty minutes like this, playfully ban-tering and cooking. Frankly, it's the most fun I've had in a kitchen in a long time.

Well, when sex wasn't involved.

"Now, we're going to ask the crew to come over here to give our dishes a taste and decide on a winner."

A cameraman, a sound person, and the makeup artist all gather around and take bites off our plates.

"Camden's wins for me."

"No, Mia's chicken is more tender."

We all stare at the makeup artist in anticipation. She grins. "Camden can cook for me any time."

And now I want to kick her in the vag, but I just smile and shake Camden's hand.

"Looks like we have a winner," I say and shrug at the camera. "If you want any of these recipes, you can find them on our home page on the Best Bites TV website. Take care, everyone."

"Cut." Trevor walks over, a wide smile on his handsome face, and pushes his glasses up his nose. "That was fantastic, you two. I don't even think we need to reshoot it."

"You're happy with one take?" Camden asks in surprise.

"I am. You were professional, but a little flirty, and there were no snafus with the food. We'll be back here again tomorrow morning to film the dessert course."

"Why are we doing them out of order?" I ask.

"Because Riley's craving sugar." He winks at us and turns away. "I'll see you both tomorrow."

I pull my hair up in a messy knot on the top of my head and sigh. "I need to wash this crap off my face. I don't want it to melt into the food today."

"That's disgusting," Camden says, wrinkling his nose. "Do you need anything?"

He's always asking me if I need anything, or want him to do something. It's sweet, and not something I'm used to.

"I don't think so. I'm going to head into the restaurant for the day."

"I have a couple of calls to make. I can come help this afternoon."

"Actually, my other chef hasn't called out yet, so I'll have plenty of help. Take the day off."

He narrows his eyes. "Really?"

"Absolutely." I stand on my tiptoes and he still has to bend down to kiss me. "I'll see you later."

Seduction isn't far from the studio. I march straight into the bathroom to wash my face before walking into the kitchen. Once I get there, all I can do is look around the room at everything I have to do.

Nothing is prepped for today yet. It's Monday, so we won't be sold out today, but I do still need to get things ready. Not to mention, someone left some dirty dishes in the dish sink, and that's never okay. My dishwasher doesn't come in until noon. There's no need for him to arrive earlier than that.

Which means I get to do some dishes.

But suddenly, as I'm standing here looking around, I realize that I'm just so fucking *tired*. We filmed for four hours this morning. We were in the studio by six, and filming by seven. I've cooked and flirted and had to turn it all on for the cameras.

And now I get to pull a full twelve-hour shift here.

I can't do it.

I turn on my heel and march into our offices, happy to see Cami sitting at her desk.

"Good morning," she says with a smile. "How was filming this morning?"

"It was actually really good." I plop down in the chair across from her and rub my hands over my face. "Camden is great in front of the camera."

"So are you." She grins and sets her spreadsheet aside. Just looking at a spreadsheet gives me hives. "What's up?"

"We need to hire someone," I reply and watch as her eyes widen in surprise. "What? I didn't just say that I want to move to Tibet."

"That's just the last thing I ever expected you to say. But I'm glad you did. Let's talk about it."

"Here's the thing. I need someone really talented. Someone who knows their shit, and that I can trust to take over the kitchen when I can't be there. It's just too much lately, with the show *and* the restaurant being as busy as we are."

"Not to mention you're trying to have a personal life," she adds with a grin. "I get it."

"Finding someone with the right skills and experience isn't going to be cheap."

"We can afford someone good," she reminds me. "We can pretty much afford whomever you want at this point."

"And isn't that amazing?" I ask. "I mean, when we started this, we just hoped that we might eventually get to a place where we could pay ourselves."

"I know. We're there and then some. So you find who you want, and we'll work out the rest."

"Thanks."

"No, thank you for finally seeing that you need the help. I've been really worried about you. The other girls will be so happy when we tell them. In fact," she checks her phone, "we should get going. We're going to be late."

"For what?"

"It's hair day at Cici's."

"I can't go to Cici's. Nothing is ready for today."

"Are you working alone?"

"No."

"Then you can go. That other chick—I can never remember their names anymore, they come and go so fast—can handle things until dinner. Your roots need some serious attention."

"They do?" I frown and touch my head. "Why didn't anyone say something?"

"Because we have an appoint today," she says with a grin.

"I'm going to be grilled."

"Oh, for sure."

I sigh and stand. "Let me make sure whatshername is really coming in today, and see if I'm needed for anything and then we can go."

"Hurry."

I roll my eyes and rush into the kitchen. Linda? Lisa? Liz? Shit, I can't remember her name either, but she's working.

"I have an appointment. Are you okay with this until dinner?"

She shrugs and looks around, nodding. "It should be fine. It's just Monday. I can do this."

"Are you sure?"

She rolls her eyes. "Mia. I can do this."

I nod. "Okay. Thank you."

I should stay. But I want to talk to my friends. I want to tell them about Camden, and get their opinions, and listen to their funny banter. So I take a deep breath, thank her again, and walk back out to find Cami waiting by the front door.

"Ready?"

"Let's go."

Cici's new shop is within walking distance from Seduction. We arrive just about ten minutes later to find Addie already getting her hair balayaged, Kat sitting in a pedicure chair with her feet soaking, and Riley getting her eyebrows waxed.

"You're here," Addie says with a smile. "I was worried that you were going to back out of girl day."

"I reminded her," Cami says and sits in the pedicure chair next to Kat. I take the empty chair next to Addie and patiently wait for my turn in Cici's chair.

Cici and Addie have been friends for years. Cici used to be Addie's hair and makeup stylist when Addie was a fashion model. Now she lives in Portland with her family and has a very successful shop, which we take over at least once a month.

"Also," Cami continues, "I am happy to report that Mia has agreed to hire another executive chef."

"Really?" Kat asks.

"Yes. I'm tired, you guys."

"You've been tired for two years," Cici reminds me.

"I know. But I think it's really caught up with me. And with the show, and our place only getting busier, I need the help. But I want someone *amazing*. So I'm going to have to do some headhunting."

"You'll find them," Riley says after coming up from having her lip waxed. "And we'll pay for them."

"That's what I said," Cami replies. "I'm so proud of you for making this decision."

The others nod in agreement. "I know I'm stubborn, and I should have made this move a year ago, but it's important to me that everything is perfect. That our guests leave after having a wonderful experience. The recipes aren't easy, and I just haven't trusted that the people we've hired could do it as well as I would."

"But it's okay to have a life outside of work," Addie says. "And maybe early on you were right to keep your own personal stamp on the menu. But we have a stellar reputation at this point, and I think it's a good time to bring in another excellent chef."

I nod, relieved that they also think it's a good idea.

"Now that that's resolved, spill it," Kat says.

"Spill what?"

"Everything," Riley adds. "Some of us know bits and pieces, but none of us knows everything, and it's about time you let your best friends in on your history with Camden and what's happening now."

"Use all the naughty words," Cami says with a nod.

I sigh and gather my thoughts. "Cami knows the history. Camden and I went to school together."

I spend the next ten minutes filling them in on everything that happened when I was twenty. School, living together, the sex, the almost pregnancy and getting married.

Leaving him.

All of it.

"Wow," Addie says with a sigh. "No wonder you freaked out when Riley said you'd be working with Camden."

I nod. "I was so embarrassed, you guys. I know I was young, and if I had it to do again I would do it *so* differently. Camden and I have talked about it. I apologized, and we've moved on."

"That's amazing," Cici says as she paints the last piece in Addie's hair and motions for me to take her place while Addie processes. "I admit, if I were Camden, I'd still be really bitter."

"Me too," I admit. "And that's why I was so apprehensive. You know how it is, if it's not part of your every day life, you can go on as if it never happened. But then suddenly, he was a part of my life again, and I didn't know how to handle it."

"It sounds like it's going well now," Addie says.

"Yeah." I grin and can feel my cheeks flush. "We're sleeping together."

"Thank God you're getting laid," Kat says. "If I'd known that getting laid would make you hire some help in the kitchen, I would have set you up long ago."

"How is the sex?" Riley asks. "I mean no disrespect by this, but Camden is fucking hot."

"I know." I wrinkle my nose. "He's *so* sexy. The sex is

amazing. It was always amazing, and now that he's all grown-up, but just . . . *wow.*"

"Good for you," Cici says and offers her fist to bump mine.

"Are you being careful?" Addie asks.

"Condoms." I shrug. "I haven't been on the pill in a long time. He takes care of it. But I had an embarrassing moment the other day."

"Tell," Cami insists.

"Well, he wanted to have shower sex."

"What is it with men and water sex?" Kat asks.

"Exactly," I reply. "And I just flat out told him that it's not exactly comfortable for a girl to have sex in the water."

"Not unless being rubbed raw is your thing," Cici says.

"It's not my thing," I say. "And he was like, really? I've never heard of that. So he just spun me around out of the water and fucked me blind."

"What's embarrassing about that?" Addie asks.

"Well, just saying something at all was awkward. No woman wants to ruin the mood and say, this isn't sexy for me."

"Screw that," Cici says, shaking her head and checking Addie's color. "I'm too damn old to have sex that hurts. I don't want to make love to my husband and spend the next week recovering from it. That's not fun."

"I agree," Riley says with a nod. "I mean, you're right, Mia. No one wants to ruin the sexy mood, but it's not worth being sore after."

"Guys just don't have the same equipment." Cami shrugs. "It's not as . . . *delicate*."

"They could fuck a porcupine and come out okay," Cici says. "Not me."

"Oh, God, speaking of porcupines," Addie says with a laugh. "Jake used to like to shave himself clean, but by later in the day, he's all stubbly down there and it felt like he was impaling me with tiny needles. I was like, go away until that shit grows out some."

"Yes!" Kat agrees. "I don't like that either. And what's up with Mac wanting to have sex *just* as I'm about to fall asleep? I'm like, you've had all damn day to attack me, and you choose the moment I'm about to fall into REM sleep."

"Oh girl, I have you beat," Addie says. "Try getting up in the middle of the night with the baby, and crawling back into bed, only to have Jake decide that since we're both awake he should just go ahead and jump on top of me."

"Ew," I say.

"Exactly. It's like, your baby just threw up all over me and I haven't had a shower in two days. I am *not* feeling romantic right now. If I get a shower in the morning, I might be able to pencil you in."

"Are we just old?" Riley asks the room at large. "I mean, ten years ago, I would have been fine with being woken up with sex. Or having it any time of day, really."

"I think it's age and being an adult," Cici says. "I'm the oldest one here, and I can say that running a business and having kids is exhausting; and unfortunately, for a long time my sex life with my husband suffered. In the last two years or so, we've made it a priority to flirt with each other and keep some spark going. Don't tell me that none of you have a spark anymore."

They all shake their heads no. "My husband is the sexiest man out there," Addie says. "And we still have amazing sex."

"I think we all have sexy, healthy men," I reply.

"They want to fuck," Kat says. "It's as simple as that. It's biology. They're built to have a lot of sex. I don't think women are, at least not quite as much."

"Just wait until you hit forty and shit starts to fall apart," Cici says. "It sucks. So enjoy your middle-of-the-night sex now."

"I don't mind middle-of-the-night sex," I reply with a grin. "The only thing that gave me pause was the water, so I guess we're doing pretty well."

"Is he sweet?" Cami asks. "He seems really sweet."

"He is. He's considerate."

"Marry him," Riley says. "Marry him right now. Sweet, considerate, sexy men are unicorns. You'll never see another one of them out in the wild. I know. I looked."

We all laugh, but I know she's right. Men like Camden are few and far between.

"I have an announcement," Cami says, changing the subject.

"Is it a good one or a bad one?" I ask.

"Oh, it's good. I'm going to have a baby."

We're quiet for a moment, and then the room explodes in

cheers and laughter and love for our sweet friend. Cami and Landon have already lost one baby to miscarriage, and she didn't know if she'd be able to get pregnant again.

"How far along are you?" Addie asks.

"Three months," she says with a soft smile. "I wanted to wait to announce it until we were out of the first trimester woods. But things are good, and I'm healthy, and I just couldn't wait anymore."

"I'm so excited for you," I say and give her a big hug. "You deserve this so much. I'm sure Landon is over the moon!"

"He's so excited," Cami says with a grin. "He's hoping for a boy, but deep down, we both just want it to be healthy and whole. Everything else is gravy."

"I couldn't agree more," Riley says. "We feel the same way."

"Wait." We all look at each other, and then back at Riley. "Are you pregnant too?"

"Two months," Riley says with a nod. "I'm sorry, I'm not trying to steal your thunder."

"Oh my God," Cami cries out and wraps Riley up in her arms. Both women are crying and laughing at the same time. "This is the best news ever!"

"So, none of us really has any true sex complaints," Cici says as she wipes a tear from her eye. "I want to throw your baby showers."

Everyone is talking at once about breastfeeding and how many weeks they have left, and bouncy seats, and I hang back, watching with so much love and excitement for them.

It's moments like this that I can't help but think *what if.*

What if I'd really been pregnant all those years ago? How different would my life be now?

But thinking that way isn't productive. And it doesn't matter. All of the most important people in my life are happy and healthy, and I've fallen in love with a man that I think I've been in love with for ten years.

I just don't know how to tell him.

Chapter Ten

~Camden~

That's a wrap for today," Trevor says. We've been filming for a week, and after every day I'm more and more impressed with Mia. She's a natural in front of the camera, and she's fun. The viewers are going to eat her up. It won't be long until she's a celebrity.

I wonder if she's thought about how she'll handle that.

"Are you okay?" she asks after she gathers her bag and keys.

"I'm great." I kiss her forehead. "How are you?"

"I'm worried about you. You have a weird look on your face."

I chuckle and shake my head. "I was just thinking about work. I have a phone call scheduled with my agent in a little bit."

"Ah, so that's your business man look." She nods. "So noted. I have interviews for the next couple of hours."

"For?"

"I'm hiring another master chef for Seduction."

"It's about time."

"Yeah, yeah. I've already heard I told you so from the girls. I'm actually more excited than I expected to be. I have some promising candidates that I'm meeting with."

"Do they live in Portland?"

"Two of them do, and one is in San Diego, but would like to move up to Portland to be closer to family, so that's a FaceTime interview."

"Well, I hope at least one of them has the experience and qualities you're looking for."

"Me too." She presses her sweet body against me and hugs me tight, then tilts her head up for a kiss. I've become completely addicted to her: The way she laughs, smells, kisses; having her naked body pressed to mine every night.

Everything.

I press my lips to hers for a short, sweet kiss. "I'll catch up with you later tonight."

"Sounds good." She grins and walks away, her heels clicking on the concrete floor. "Have a good day!"

She has a new bounce in her step that wasn't there a week ago. I wonder if it has anything to do with me.

I hurry back to my rental and just as I sit at my computer my agent's FaceTime comes in.

"Hey, Don."

"Camden." He smiles when he sees me. Don's been an entertainment agent for a long time. He's nearing retirement age, with white hair and a saggy face. He's a grandfather, but he's as entrenched in the entertainment industry as he ever was, and he's been an excellent agent for me.

Hell, without him I wouldn't have the hit TV show, or the several millions of dollars that comes with it each season.

"How are things in Portland?" he asks.

"They're good. We're filming this week for the pilot." He nods and looks down at something on his desk.

"Good to hear. When will you be back in L.A.?"

"I'm not sure."

Don frowns. "What do you mean? You should be wrapped on filming next week."

"I know, but I'm not contractually required to be back on set for another month, so I'm taking some personal time."

"I'm sorry, I need to speak with Camden Sawyer please."

I smirk. "You're a riot, Don. What's up?"

"Well, I would rather speak to you about all of this in person, but this will do. I heard back from Best Bites TV, and they've decided to pass on any more seasons of your show."

"We're under contract for one more season."

"They're aware, and have decided to buy out the last season on your contract rather than shoot more episodes."

"Why are they unhappy?"

"I don't think it's a matter of being unhappy with *you*," he says, and I can see that he's telling the truth. "In fact, I know that they'll come back with something new for you. Of course, I don't know what that is at this time. Your career isn't over, Cam, they just weren't as happy with last season's numbers as they have been in the past."

"So they're going to pay me anyway?"

"Absolutely. They're under contract to pay you. You didn't do anything wrong, and this is *their* decision. Otherwise, we would sue the hell out of them."

"Then I guess I don't have to be back in L.A. in a month."

"I'm working on getting you other gigs. I know that I could get you on as a guest judge on *Chopped*. Not to mention, there have been several requests from restaurants all over the country to have you as a guest chef for a week at a time or so. You know, if Emeril goes on vacation, someone still has to cook at the restaurant."

"I get it," I reply with a nod, but none of that sounds particularly exciting to me right now. "Feel free to call me if something firms up, but I'm happy where I am right now. I'm in no hurry to come back to L.A."

"Camden," Don says, his face turning paternal and concerned. "I'm going to find you work."

"I'm not worried," I reply, surprised to find it true.

"You work harder than anyone I know. Being idle for long won't sit well with you," he says.

"I appreciate your help," I say.

I keep the rest of the conversation short and hang up, wondering why I'm not more worried than I am. At the end of the day, I'm unemployed. Well, aside from this job with Mia, but that's not supposed to be long term.

I've been in television for eight years, and it's been good to me. It's not only made me wealthy, it's made Camden Sawyer a household name thanks to my own cookware line and a line of sauces in national grocery stores.

I've worked my ass off most of my life. I call Stephanie to get her take on things.

"Whatcha doing?" she asks as she answers the FaceTime.

"Calling you." She wrinkles her nose at me. "So, I just got off the phone with Don, and I think he's concerned."

"Well, I've always thought he was a dick, so there's that."

"He's a dick who got me some pretty good gigs, so there's also that."

"And in doing so, he not only made you rich, he made himself rich too."

"Well, that's his job." I shake my head and watch as Chip kisses Steph's cheek as he walks by. "Hi, Chip."

"Hey man," he says with a smile. "I don't think Don's a dick."

"Maybe it's a girl thing," I reply, earning a glare from Steph.

"I'm telling you, he's smarmy. I don't like him."

"It's okay. You don't have to like him." Chip kisses her cheek again, waves at me, and walks out of camera range.

"I have some interesting news."

"Okay."

I tell her about the network passing on any more seasons of my show, and the other possibilities that Don and I discussed.

"At least you'll still get paid," she says. "But what are you going to do?"

"I don't know. And the thing is, Steph, I don't know if I care."

"What do you mean?"

"I'm not worried in the least. I know that I can do the guest appearance thing from time to time. That doesn't sound bad at all."

"But it's not full time."

I shake my head and push my hand through my hair. "I just love the idea of not being under a contract for a while. There's a lot of pressure involved with the contract. I have to maintain a certain look."

"Are you going to let yourself go?"

"No. But if I decide I don't want to shave for a week, I don't have to. There's really no pressure, and it's a nice change.

"Not to mention, I've been telling Mia for the past two weeks that she's too much of a control freak when it comes to work. She works too hard and too long, and that she should be able to relax a bit."

"Did she introduce you to the kettle?"

"Exactly. I'm the same. I've worked hard for *years*, and I've been rewarded handsomely. I don't want to retire. But it's okay to slow down a bit, isn't it? To actually enjoy what I've earned?"

"I don't see why not."

"I mean, I could make Portland home base, and if I get called for guest appearances, I can travel. And who says I have to stay in show business? I could teach."

"Wait. Back it up. You want to stay in Portland? Talk to me, Cam."

I look up at the ceiling and rub my fingers over my lips. "Mia's pretty incredible."

"Are you . . . What are you doing, exactly?"

"You don't want to know what, exactly, we're doing."

"Yuck."

I laugh and then shrug. "Am I stupid?"

"Yes." Her eyes are full of humor and love as she smiles at me. "Okay, you're not really stupid. But I need more information."

"When it comes to Mia, I'm just . . . well, I'm enamored by her. She makes me laugh, she challenges me. She's so beautiful."

"You're falling in love with her," she says, and I pause.

"I care about her."

"I know, Camden Sawyer doesn't use the *L* word." She rolls her eyes and sighs deeply. "But that's what this is, Cam."

"Am I stupid?" I ask again.

"Why are you asking me that?"

"Because I'm investing a lot of myself into this again. I couldn't stop myself if I wanted to, Steph. It's as if I'm *supposed* to be with her. But I also can't help but wonder if I'm just a chump. I mean, she could run again. Maybe not tomorrow, or even next week. But there could come a day when I come home and she's *gone*. And I don't know if I would survive it again. I hate how weak I sound saying that, but it's true."

"Have your communication skills improved?" she asks gently. "That's never been your strong suit."

"Just because I don't tell everyone that I love them all the time doesn't mean I don't show them that I care. Actions speak louder than words, remember?"

"A woman needs the words, Camden," she says. "Whether you believe it or not, she does. You didn't say it long ago, and she thought that meant that you didn't care if she stayed or left. It's as simple as that. I'm not saying you should say it if you don't mean it, but if you *do* mean it, what's the harm? Why is it so fucking hard for you? I tell you I love you all the time, but I don't think you've ever said it back to me."

"Of course I love you," I reply with frustration. Tears spring to her eyes, and I feel like a grade A asshole. "Steph, you know I love you."

"But there's nothing like hearing it," she replies. "I don't know how Mia feels. I have no way of knowing what's going on in her head. Could she bail? Sure. Anyone could, Cam. You really need to talk to Mia about this. Especially if you're considering a move to Portland. I wouldn't do that until you've defined what this relationship is."

"I would marry her again tomorrow," I reply truthfully. "She's an exceptional woman."

"I'm happy for you," she says. "I truly am. Maybe the time is right now. Maybe you both needed to grow up and experience some life so you'd appreciate each other even more when you finally found each other again."

"Now you're making it sound like a movie."

"Hey, I like a good rom-com." She smiles. "Since the job thing isn't a financial issue for you, and it really is all about this woman and what may or may not come of your relationship with her, you need to have a conversation. You might even have to use the L word, Cam."

"Yeah." I sigh and push my fingers through my hair again. "You're right. You know, I don't know why it's hard for me to use that word."

"I'm not a shrink, but I suspect it has to do with Mom and Dad dying. And some people are just not good at using their words." She shrugs. "I don't know. But if you're going to be with Mia, you're going to have to tell her how you feel."

"Okay. Thanks for listening, Dr. Steph."

"You're welcome. Keep me posted. This is better than TV."

"I'm happy to entertain." I end the call and glance at the clock. Mia still has a long workday ahead, and I want to talk to her *right now*. Not gonna happen. So instead I head to the gym for the first time in more than a week to work off some of my aggression, and figure out what I'm going to say to Mia later tonight.

I HAVEN'T SEEN Mia since this morning, and I miss her. Today was productive, however. I spent two hours at the gym, and I felt better than ever when I was finished. No more skipping exercise.

I caught up on laundry and paid bills. I spoke with my CPA.

I received a call from a woman that I casually dated for a time in L.A., and had the unpleasant task of telling her to not call me anymore.

She wasn't pleased.

I didn't give a fuck.

And then I got to work baking Mia's favorite cheesecake and ordering flowers to be delivered to the restaurant.

The cheesecake took all fucking day. The recipe is challenging and time consuming, but it always turns out better than if I try to cut corners with a simpler recipe. This is her favorite, so this is what she'll have.

At around nine thirty, I send her a text and ask her to let me know when she's home. I could meet her at Seduction, but I'll still have to follow her home. This is easier.

At ten thirty, I get a reply.

Just walked in the door. Is everything okay?

She's a thoughtful woman. An empathetic one. She takes on the feelings of those around her, and I know that it just adds to her stress. As much as she'd like everyone to think she's a grouchy hard-ass, that actually couldn't be farther from the truth.

Everything is fine. I'm going to head your way.

A second later she replies with, *The door is unlocked.*

I load up the cake and make it to her place in record time. I'm excited to see her.

I'm whipped.

I knock once on the door and then open it, smiling at Mia, who's curled up in the corner of her couch. She's grinning sleepily.

"What do you have there?" she asks.

"Cheesecake."

Her eyes widen in surprise and hope. "The super hard one you learned to make in school?"

"That's the one."

"Oh my God." She jumps up and practically yanks it out of my hands, then lifts her face up for a kiss. "Thank you."

"I didn't say it's for you."

"You'd better plan on sharing," she replies as she walks ahead of me to the kitchen. "Also, thank you *so much* for the beautiful flowers today. They were a fun treat, too."

"Where are they?"

"In the bedroom." She smiles as she pulls two plates out of the cupboard. "I want to smell them in there."

"I didn't know if you were a flower lover. Some women think they're a waste of money."

"I'm not one of those women. You've seen my garden." She holds a knife over the cake and looks back at me. "Is it okay if I cut this?"

"I made it to be eaten."

"Well, maybe you didn't intend for me to eat it *tonight*."

"That would be cruel and unusual to bring it over and expect you to wait until tomorrow to eat it. I'm not a monster."

"Oh thank God," she says and cuts us each a piece, slides them onto plates, and passes me mine with a fork. "Is this salted caramel on top?"

"Of course."

"You're spoiling me," she says with a smile and takes a bite. "You've gotten even better at this."

I set my plate aside without taking a bite, happy to watch her eat hers. I lean my hips against the counter and cross my arms over my chest. "You're beautiful, Mia."

She pauses mid-bite, the fork still in her mouth, and watches me for a moment; then resumes, chewing on the cake. "Something's up with you today."

"There's nothing up. Really."

"Flowers. Cheesecake. Telling me I'm beautiful."

"Because you *are* beautiful."

She frowns and looks back down at her cake, then sets

it aside and wipes her mouth on a napkin. Without a word, she walks to me and hugs me tightly. My arms circle around her and I hold on.

"There's something off with you tonight. Are you sure you're okay?"

"I am," I reply and kiss her head. "I just needed to hold you. And maybe do something nice for you today. You deserve it."

She leans back and smiles up at me. Her face has softened, and I can see it written all over her gorgeous face.

She loves me.

And I love her too.

"How was your day?"

"I had an awesome day," she says. "I hired someone. This super-sexy guy I know sent me flowers and made me cheesecake. I mean, it doesn't get better than that."

"I'm glad." I back her up until she's caged against the counter and bury my face in her neck. "I need you tonight, Mia."

"I'm right here," she says, burying her fingers in my hair. Her hands glide soothingly down my back and up again. "I'm right here."

I take her hand and lead her to her bedroom. Just as she reaches to pull her shirt over her head, I stop her. "Wait."

"What?"

"Tonight is about going slow."

"We always take it slow, Cam."

"I guess we do. I enjoy taking my time with you." I drag my thumb down her cheek to her lips. She sticks her tongue out, brushing the pad of my thumb, and it makes my dick stand at attention. "Taking it fast would be such a waste."

"Why?"

"Because then I wouldn't get to see this."

Chapter Eleven

~Mia~

The way he looks at me makes the tiny hairs all over my body stand on end. His eyes are on fire as he looks me up and down, still clothed, and his hands travel down my arms to hold my hands.

"What do you see?" I whisper.

"Your body come alive," he says. "The more turned on you get, the faster you breathe. Your cheeks flush. You bite that fucking sexy bottom lip of yours."

I grin and do exactly that, then let my head fall back and moan when his hands travel under my shirt. His hands glide up my sides and he cups my breasts over my bra.

"Your nipples harden."

"Of course they do," I reply as if in a trance. "You're touching them."

His eyes narrow as he pulls my shirt up over my head

and drops it to the floor beside us. He slips a finger under my bra strap and tugs it to the side, then kisses me there.

"Your skin is so damn soft."

His eyes are pinned to mine as he slowly and methodically peels me out of my clothes. I'm standing here—naked as can be—and he's clearly turned on by it, if the bulge against his jeans is any indication.

"Soft skin," he murmurs again. "Gorgeous curves. Amazing smile." He moves closer and kisses me while his hands slide down my back to my ass. He slips a finger down my ass and finds my wet core. "I fucking love your pussy."

"As you can see, it loves you too." I grin as he sheds his clothes and reaches out for me. We tumble onto the bed, but rather than let him cover me, I push his shoulder back and climb on top of him. I straddle him and rub myself against his hard cock, reveling in how amazing he feels against my wetness.

"Fucking hell, Mia," he moans. His hands are on my hips, but I'm controlling the movement. I know he wants to take it slow, so I move deliberately and smile in satisfaction when he sucks a breath in through his gritted teeth.

"Do you like that?"

"Fuck." I reach for a condom, take my time rolling it over the length of him, then rise up and take just the tip inside of me, clench my muscles, and then slide all the way down until he's impaled me completely. "Jesus, baby."

I lean down and kiss him. His hands cup my jaw, and his hips begin to move with mine.

"You just . . . I—"

He closes his eyes and shakes his head.

"I don't know how to say it."

"Don't say it," I reply and begin to ride him faster now. *I think this man loves me.* I can see it in his eyes when he looks at me. When he laughs with me. When he touches me.

All day long, it felt like he was telling me he loves me. The flowers, delicate pink peonies, were perfect. His sweet text messages, asking me if I'm having a good day. The selfie he sent me from the gym, which I admit completely turned me on. The cheesecake.

I just can't ask for more than that.

The room is warm and bathed in low light from my lamp. His eyes are pinned to mine as I move at a faster pace now, enjoying the way he feels. How he makes *me* feel. He finds my clit with his thumb, and I'm done for. Every muscle in my body tightens, my skin tingles as I come apart. He pulls me down on him, firmly grinding against me, as he comes with me.

I fall onto the bed beside him to catch my breath. He chuckles and rolls to his side, his head braced on his hand and smiles down at me.

"That was fun."

"Oh yeah." I nod and reach for the covers.

"Are you cold? I think it's hot in here."

"It's warm," I agree. "But I'm naked and the lights are on."

He rolls his eyes and flings the covers away. "I've seen it all, and I love it all. No need to cover up unless you're cold."

I turn on my side to face him. "You're very bossy in bed."

"Always have been," he agrees. "Does it bother you?"

"You would think it would," I say thoughtfully. "I don't usually like to be told what to do."

"You're an independent woman," he says, but not in a mocking or condescending way.

"Yes, and I can be bossy too. But I don't mind at all when you take over in the bedroom."

"What about the bathroom? Or the kitchen?"

He's got his smart-ass smile on. "In any room you like."

"That's my girl," he says and kisses me thoroughly, then turns to rid himself of the condom and turn off the light. He tucks me against him and kisses my head. "Sleep, beautiful Mia."

"I'm not sleepy," I reply in the middle of a yawn.

"Right." He kisses my forehead.

"I like lying on your chest. It isn't too hairy."

"Good to know."

I smile, but he can't see me in the dark. I drape my leg over his and kiss his shoulder. My eyes *are* heavy. His breathing has evened out, and I'm quite sure he's already fallen asleep.

Typical.

But honestly, I could lie here all night and just listen to the sound of his heart and his breathing. His skin is smooth against my cheek, and his body is firm and warm. I didn't know that I was craving touch so badly until Camden came back into my life.

Now I don't know what I would do without it. I don't want to think about that. I know that he'll be leaving soon, and I don't know for sure what will happen after that. I guess we'll cross that bridge when we get to it.

Soon I realize that I'm sleepier than I thought.

"WHY DOES HE need to see us *right now*?" I ask Camden the next morning. It's not even nine yet, on a Saturday no less, and I wasn't ready to go to the restaurant. I had at least another hour of lazy time coming to me.

"He didn't say," Camden says. He reaches over to lay his hand on my thigh. This man never stops touching me.

And I'm not complaining.

"He just said that he needed to meet with us. I think he's invited everyone."

"Shit. They've cancelled the show." I rub my fingertips against my forehead. "His bosses didn't like it. This sucks so bad. He moved here for this show. I mean, he really moved here for Riley, but it was possible for him to do so because of this show. If he can't work here, what will happen? Riley will be crushed if she has to move back to L.A. That can't happen, Cam."

"Whoa. Slow down, control freak—(a) he didn't sound upset at all; and (b) you are taking on everyone else's stress, and that's not healthy."

"That's who I am," I reply and stare out the passenger window as Portland breezes by. "She'll be devastated. God, this sucks."

"You're such an optimist," Camden says and glances at me with a worried frown. "Seriously, stop that. It's probably something completely different."

I nod, but I don't think that's the case at all. I have a bad feeling about this.

Shit. Poor Riley.

Camden pulls up to the restaurant and I trudge inside. I didn't put on any makeup this morning. By the time Trevor called and said he needed to see us ASAP, there just wasn't time.

I also haven't had a whole cup of coffee yet, and that is never okay.

The others are already sitting in the dining room, at two round tables that have been pushed together.

"Who brought muffins?" I ask as I snatch one and take a seat. "We haven't had breakfast yet."

"Or coffee, from the looks of it," Cami says with a sweet smile. I narrow my eyes on her as I take a bite of my muffin.

"This is store bought," I say. "But it's not too bad."

"Of course it's store bought," Addie says. "Unless *you* make them from scratch, this is what we get."

"At least I know I serve a purpose."

The others smirk as Trevor stands, holding an iPad. "Thanks for coming everyone. I know it's unusual to meet about business matters on a Saturday, but I wanted to bring this to your attention right away."

My eyes are pinned to Riley. Does she already know?

"A few days ago, I submitted the film that we had already shot to my boss. I wouldn't usually do that, but I saw something there that I wanted *him* to see. And he agrees with me. We've decided to switch things up."

"I'm so sorry," I whisper and cover my face with my hands.

"Why are you sorry?" Addie asks from across the table.

"Obviously he's about to tell us that the show has been cancelled already."

"Oh please," Cami says, rolling her eyes.

"Well, she's not entirely wrong," Trevor says. I cover my face again and shake my head. *I've screwed this up for them.* "But she's not right either. Camden and Mia, you two work exceptionally well in front of the camera. You're fun to watch. The flirting is natural, and both of you are attractive people.

"The more I watched, the more obvious it became to me that you shouldn't be working *against* each other, you should be a team. My boss just called me about an hour ago, and gave me the thumbs-up on this. Unfortunately, that means that we'll have to reshoot what we've done so you're not in competition with each other, but rather working together."

"But, Camden has a job," I say, confused.

"Actually," Trevor says, "Best Bites TV has decided not to shoot any more seasons of his current show."

"What?" I turn to Camden and can see that he's already aware of this. "Why didn't you tell me?"

"I just found out about it yesterday," he replies, staring at Trevor. "How did *you* know?"

"You're on my show, Camden. Of course I know. This is one of the reasons that your show wasn't picked up again."

"Oh God." I sigh and look at Camden apologetically. "I'm so sorry."

He just shakes his head. I can tell that he's agitated. I could see it on him last night when he arrived at my house. This must be what was bothering him.

"I think this show is going to be amazing," Riley says with a smile. "Trevor ran it by me last night before he'd heard back, and I agree that viewers are going to love you guys."

"You didn't tell me?" I ask.

"Mia, I couldn't say anything until Trevor had the green light. If they didn't go for it, there was no need to mention it."

"So what do you think?" Trevor asks, looking at all of us. Kat, Cami, and Addie all nod.

"It's really up to Mia and Camden," Kat says. "They're the ones who will be working together. The show benefits the restaurant, there's no denying that, but the specifics are up to you guys."

"Agreed," Addie says.

Trevor looks at Camden and me. "What do you two think?"

"I need some time with Mia," Camden says before I can respond.

"Of course," Riley says, standing. The others follow suit and they all wander into the bar.

"What do you think?" he asks me after they're out of the room.

"I think I'm surprised," I reply truthfully. "And I'm disappointed that you didn't mention the change with your show last night."

"I had better things to do," he says with a smile.

"Really, you're the one that has to decide if you want to do this," I say. "You're the one who will have to spend a chunk of time in Portland. My life really isn't disrupted either way."

"Okay, let me ask you this way. Do you *want* to work with me on a full-time basis?"

I frown and consider how much to say. Of *course* I want him here full time. The thought of him leaving makes me break out in hives.

But I don't know if we're ready for that kind of truth yet.

"Mia, you have to talk to me here."

"I would be fine with it," I reply. "Shooting the show with you last week was fun. I can see why Trevor wants to change things up this way. I just want to know how you feel."

"Honestly, we would have had this conversation soon anyway, Trevor just beat me to the punch. I'd like to make Portland my home base for a while. I just got you back in my life, and I'm not ready to lose you again this soon. This show would be the perfect way for me to stay here."

I smile, hope blooming in my chest. "You'd already thought about this?"

"I had. We would have had this exact talk within the next forty-eight hours, I promise you."

"I'm definitely not ready to say good-bye to you." I brush a strand of hair from my cheek. "I think this show would be fun. I'm in if you're in."

"Let's call Trevor back and tell him it's a go." He smiles and kisses my cheek. "Thank you."

"Were you surprised during the meeting yesterday?" Addie asks me the following afternoon. We're in downtown Portland shopping—at my request.

I don't know what's gotten into me.

"I was worried that we'd been cancelled," I reply and check out a black top. "But *not* being cancelled was a nice surprise."

"Of course you're not cancelled. You're too good in front of the camera."

I roll my eyes, but Addie keeps talking.

"I'm serious. I've been in front of the camera most of my life, and I know when someone has *it*. And you have it, my friend."

"Well, thanks. And thanks for coming with me today. I usually hate to shop."

"I know. Are you sick?"

"No." I laugh and hold up a bright pink pair of pants. "I need help from the fashionista."

"I'm your girl," she says, and shakes her head no at the pink pants. "Put those down right now. Don't even look at them again."

"Yes ma'am." I hold my arms out at my sides and look around. "I don't know where to start. I usually just buy stuff that isn't tight and is easy to wash."

"This is painful," she says, pinching the bridge of her nose. "Okay, today is going to be a lesson in fashion. Now that you'll be on TV full time, we need to revamp your wardrobe. Are you going to have someone do your wardrobe for the show?"

"I don't think so," I reply.

"Okay great. You can write most of this off on your taxes, since you'll be wearing it on air. We're going to start with pants, then tops and dresses. We'll end our day with shoes and bags because that's my favorite part, so we'll consider it dessert."

"Is this going to take a long time?"

"Do you have something else to do?" She raises a brow.

"I have a date with Camden at seven."

"We'll be done by then, and you'll have a sexy new outfit to rock on that date. Trust me."

"I do." She leads me into the plus-sized section of Nordstrom and starts looking through racks and racks of jeans. She pulls out four pairs of jeans, two pairs of cropped pants, and moves on to tops.

By the time she's done, the dressing room is filled with every fabric and color there is. Addie takes a seat on the bench outside the dressing room and points at me. "Go try them on."

"All of them?"

"All of them."

I roll my eyes and shut the door, looking around me. She's organized them by outfit, thank God. Otherwise, I never would be able to pair them up.

I try on several outfits that she likes, but she doesn't love.

"Try the black-and-white striped cold shoulder top next."

"Why do I want my shoulders to be cold?"

She laughs and shrugs. "Because it's cute."

I try on the one she wants and walk out to look in the mirror. "Oh, I like this. I have a waist."

"Exactly," she says with a nod, standing next to me. "See, it's not a sack. We don't lose you in there. It hugs you where you want to show off, and it camouflages the spots we don't want to draw attention to.

"Now, we'll add a pair of ripped cropped pants, and this look is *so cute*."

I add the pants and can't help but agree with her. The outfit is flattering and fun.

"These jeans are one hundred dollars," I say, blinking quickly.

"Yep, and you're buying them."

I scowl and return to the dressing room. When I come out in another outfit, I shake my head no. "I don't like it."

"Why? It's adorable on you. And the white looks fantastic with your dark hair."

"It's too tight on me."

"It doesn't look too tight. Remember, the baggy clothes aren't flattering, Mia. If you don't want to accentuate your weight, you can't wear clothes that make you look *bigger*."

"Says the fashion model."

"Hey, I'm not a tiny girl either. Look at this." She pulls her shirt up under her boobs. "I have a fat roll, and stretch marks from Ella. My hips are *ridiculous*. But I know how to dress so those aren't the things you see. Trust me when I say, I don't see the weight when you wear this. I see a beautiful, confident woman."

"I guess I'm just used to always wearing baggy things."

"I know, and it'll take some getting used to. But you really do look amazing. I wouldn't let you walk out of here in anything less."

We choose about ten outfits and three dresses. My credit card is weeping as we move on to shoes and bags.

"Addie, I'm not paying this much for a handbag."

She rolls her eyes again. "Mia, you've carried the same handbag since college. It's not cute. It's not even sort of cute. You carry a handbag every day. I'm not even asking you to buy a Chanel bag. Let's start with Coach or Michael Kors. Kate Spade is adorable. They're affordable too."

She's right. They are cute, and spending a couple hundred dollars on one is much better than spending the several thousand dollars that I know she and Cami spend on bags.

"You know, I was going to buy knives. I need knives. Instead I've bought more clothes than I've ever had in my whole life combined."

"You don't need more knives. You have a million of them. Stop pouting."

"I like knives."

"And you'll love these shoes." She hands me several pairs to try on. "How are things with Camden?"

"Really good." I bite my lip as I slide my feet into the cutest black shoes I've ever seen. "I can't wear these at work."

"No, those are for dates with Camden," she says with a wink. "Men like a girl in sexy shoes. And they don't always have to be heels to be sexy."

"Thank God because I'd fall and kill myself."

"No you wouldn't. But I know you like the flats. Tell me more about Camden."

"He's a nice guy. I don't know if there's more to say that

you don't already know. But it's going well, and he makes me happy."

"Good. That's all any of us want for you, sweetie." She smiles and piles up the boxes that we'll be taking with us. "We did well today."

"Shopping with you is expensive."

"Well"—she smiles shyly—"thank you for the compliment."

I snort and follow her to the check out. "Good-bye, knives."

"I know how much money you make. You can still buy the knives."

Chapter Twelve

~Camden~

I've never seen her like this. I've seen her laugh before, but not like *this*.

We're at a comedy show in Portland that's been sold out for weeks, but I pulled some strings and here we are. Third table back from the stage, we're enjoying dinner and a drink while some comedian named Iliza talks about how women love fall, and all things pumpkin, and pinning nonsense on Pinterest.

Mia is laughing her ass off. Nodding. I take a photo of her just as she wipes a tear from the corner of her eye.

The show is just over an hour, and by the time it's finished, Mia looks all worn out.

"She's funny," I say and enjoy my after-dinner drink.

"Oh my God, *so* funny," she replies and sips her water. "I haven't laughed that hard in a long time."

"You're gorgeous when you laugh," I inform her casually. Her eyes widen slightly and then she shrugs one shoulder, almost letting the compliment roll off her. "And your outfit is sexy as fuck. Did you go shopping?"

She nods happily. "Addie and I went this afternoon. She destroyed my bank account, but I figured that it was time for a wardrobe rehab. Especially since I'll be on television more, and Addie is the best person to take shopping. She knows what she's doing."

"I have to agree. You look beautiful." I lean in and kiss her bare shoulder. "Why is there a hole in the shirt where your shoulders go?"

"Because it's the style," she says with a laugh. "I think it's supposed to be mysterious and alluring. Like, I'm going to be demure, but just in case you forgot, I have skin too. Here, I'll show you just a little of it. On my shoulder."

I'm laughing now and can't resist leaning back in to kiss the shoulder in question. "It's working. I definitely have a desire to see the rest of the skin that the shirt is hiding."

"Awesome, my plan is working." She wiggles her eyebrows and finishes her water. "What should we do next?"

"Well, I was thinking about walking across the street to go dancing." Her eyes light up like it's Christmas morning. "I know you like to dance in the kitchen. Do you like to dance *out* of the kitchen?"

"Hell yes," she says, nodding enthusiastically. She reaches for her purse. "Let's go."

The club across the street is busy, but given that it's a Sunday evening, it's not crammed. The music is thumping, much too loud to have a conversation, which is just fine with me. I don't plan to do much talking. The moment we walk through the door, Mia's body is moving with the beat of the music. Her handbag is small, and slips over her head to hang across her body, resting on her hip. With her hands free, she grins and leads me out onto the dance floor.

She has great rhythm, and when her hips begin to move, I'm transfixed. This could have been a very bad idea. I could conceivably embarrass myself.

I'm that turned on.

I begin to move with the music too, and Mia smiles widely.

"You can dance!" she exclaims. I just nod and take her hand, spin her away from me, then pull her close and enjoy the fuck out of her.

It's vertical sex. We're lost in a sea of bodies, moving together, letting the pounding music pulse around us and through us. She has no inhibitions at all. No insecurities.

She's having a blast, and there's nowhere else I'd rather be than right here with her.

Suddenly, a younger dude comes up behind her, sandwiching her between us and grinding on her ass. She smirks up at me, then turns around and says, "You're not invited to this party, cowboy."

Instead of getting mad, the kid laughs and dances away, and Mia returns to me. She only has eyes for me, and it makes me feel like the most powerful man in the world.

The DJ seamlessly changes the song and we spend the next two hours dancing without a break.

"Do you need some water?" I yell at her, but she just smiles and shakes her head no.

"Later," she mouths and keeps shaking those hips. I'm going to fuck her from behind tonight, holding on to those hips. I reach for them now and pull her against me. She can feel my hard-on against her back, and she smiles up at me with pure female satisfaction.

I lower my lips to her ear.

"You fucking turn me on."

She laughs and reaches up to cup my face in her palm, dancing against me. Jesus, how can she do this for so long? I'm exhausted, and I work out regularly.

But then it occurs to me—so does she. She's used to standing in her kitchen for sometimes fifteen hours in a day. Of course dancing for a few hours isn't difficult for her.

I'm shocked when the DJ suddenly comes over the mic and says, "Well, party people, this is the last song for tonight. You don't have to go home, but you can't stay here. Be good out there."

The house lights come up. Mia's face is sweaty and happier than I've seen her.

"Are you ready to go home?" I ask.

She shakes her head. "Absolutely not."

"Okay." I laugh and lead her outside of the club. The cool night air feels amazing. Mia's fanning her face with her hand, but she's still smiling and breathing hard.

"That was so fucking fun," she says. "Thank you. Maybe the best date I've ever been on in my life."

"Wow, that's a lot of pressure. Now I can never outdo this one."

"You'll figure something out," she says with a shrug. "That felt fantastic."

"Do you go out dancing often?" I ask as I take her hand in mine, thread our fingers, and walk with her toward my car.

"Not as often as I'd like," she confesses. "The girls and I go out sometimes, but this was long overdue."

"We'll have to make a point to go more often." I open the door for her and she smiles up at me.

"I'd like that."

The street lights are shining on her, making her eyes and face glow, and I can't resist her. I pin her against the car and lean in, pressing the length of me against her. Kissing her like my life fucking depends on it.

Because right now it feels like it does. Nothing in my life has ever compared to the way I feel when I'm with this woman.

Her hands are fisted in my shirt on my sides as I cup her face and take and take.

"Get a room!" Someone shouts, bringing me out of the cloud of lust surrounding us.

I pull back and drag my knuckles down her cheek. She's still breathing hard, but from the kiss now rather than the dancing.

"What do you want to do now?" I'm expecting her to say go home and get naked. I'm not expecting what comes next.

"French fries." She grins. "I want French fries and maybe some pie. I think I've earned them."

"Fuck yes, you have." She lowers herself into my car and I walk around it to join her. "Where should we go for our late-night snack?"

"There's an all-night diner about eight blocks from here." She points the way she wants me to go, and I follow. "I had no idea you could dance like that."

"I, too, am a mystery." She laughs and reaches over to take my hand, which gives me pause. This might be the first time she's ever grabbed my hand. It's usually the other way around. "I knew a long time ago that the best way to impress a woman was to be able to dance. Most men don't. So, you can take me out in public—to clubs, or weddings—and be proud of the way I dance."

"That's slick," she says with a satisfied nod. "And makes me happy because dancing is fun."

She points to the diner, and I snag a parking space right out front. "It's busy."

"It usually is," she says with a nod. "Not many places are open twenty-four hours anymore. And this place has been here forever. They're a staple."

The diner is old-fashioned. White tables are surrounded by red booths. There's a vintage jukebox in the corner. The lunch counter is white with red stools, and it looks like they make old-fashioned milk shakes and sodas.

"I feel like I just stepped back in time by about fifty years."

"Exactly." We sit in a corner booth, across from each

other. I immediately take her hand in mine as the waitress approaches with menus and glasses of water. Her name tag says Flo.

"Something to drink?"

"Just water," Mia says. I nod, wanting the same and we both set the menus aside. "We're ready to order."

"What can I getcha?"

"A big order of French fries." Mia grins. "And what kind of pie do you have?"

Flo lists off about a half dozen pies and Mia licks her lips. "I'm going to think about it while I eat the fries."

"You're my kinda girl," Flo says with a wink, then walks away.

"I'm surprised that you're not tired."

"I know." She brushes her hair off her shoulder; then reaches in her pocket for a black elastic, which she uses to twist her mane up off her neck and out of her way. "That's better. I should be tired. Addie dragged me all over downtown Portland today. I'm not complaining because it was fun. I don't usually get to hang out with the girls one-on-one. If we have time away from Seduction, we like to hang out as a group.

"So, shopping through town was a great way to catch up."

"What else did you do today?" I ask.

"We had lunch. Then we hauled all of my new things home, and she insisted that she come inside to help me weed through my closet. I needed to throw some things away, give some to charity, and make room for all of the new pretties."

"Jesus, how much did you buy?"

"Way more than I planned to," she says with a laugh. "But it's fun. The clothes make me feel good, so why not, you know?" She shrugs. "Life's too short to wear bad clothes."

"That sounds like something Addie would say."

"Oh, she said it about fourteen times today."

Our fries are delivered along with sides of ketchup and ranch dressing, and Mia dives in. "Mm, salty goodness. Eat some."

"I plan to." I take my phone out of my pocket and snap a photo of her taking a bite of a fry.

"You take a lot of photos."

"Does it bother you?"

"No."

Her eyes are starting to get droopy. "Are you getting tired?"

"A little." She smiles softly and eats her fries. "It's because I sat down."

"We can go."

"Not without pie." She finishes her fries and flags Flo down. "I'll take a slice of the cherry pie to go."

Flo nods and walks away to fetch Mia's treat and our tab. Ten minutes later, we're driving toward her house. It doesn't take nearly as long to get there in the middle of the night with no traffic.

"I'm going to take a quick shower to get this sweat off," she says.

"Good idea. I'm going to take one in your guest bathroom, if that's okay."

"Sounds efficient to me," she says with a grin. "There are fresh towels and soap in there."

While she's in the shower, I plate her pie and get a fork, set them on her nightstand with half of a glass of her favorite wine, then go to take my own shower.

I'd join her, but we're both exhausted. And as much as she turns me on, and all I want is to be buried deep inside of her, I'm also looking forward to snuggling up to her tonight.

I've never been this guy. I'm not the guy that stays and snuggles all night. It's never interested me.

And now you couldn't get me to leave with all of the money in the world.

When I walk into Mia's bedroom, naked except for the towel that I'm currently drying my hair with, she's just slipping between the covers.

"Thanks for this," she says, gesturing to the pie and wine. "I'll sleep for a week if I drink this."

"I think you'll probably sleep for a week without it."

She shrugs. "Probably." She picks up her plate and takes a bite. "Oh God. I know I shouldn't eat this right before I go to sleep, but holy Moses, it tastes good."

"Can I have a bite?"

She looks uncertain. "I guess."

She offers me a small bite and I raise an eyebrow at her. "Really?"

"You want me to *share* this pie?"

"Yes."

"Camden, you totally could have also purchased a slice of pie."

"I purchased *this* slice of pie," I remind her.

"For me."

"For us."

She narrows her eyes and slips my tiny bite of pie in her own mouth, chewing slowly as if she's considering what to do.

God, she's funny.

"You know you want to share."

"Or, you know, I *don't* want to share." She shrugs and takes another bite, making me laugh.

"Fine. Keep the pie. I had no idea you were so selfish."

She grins and offers me a big bite, which I take and immediately nod in agreement. "Okay. I get it. I wouldn't want to share either."

"I'll share with you. Because you're nice, and handsome, and you bought it for me."

"Your kindness is acknowledged and appreciated."

Three bites later, the pie is gone, the plate set aside, and we're scooting down in bed. I pull her against me, the way I've become accustomed to in the past few weeks since being with her again. Her head is on my chest, her arm and leg both draped around me.

"Are you comfy?" she asks softly.

"Oh yeah."

"Do we want to do the sex tonight?"

I smirk. "*The sex*? No. I don't think I could muster up the energy right now."

"Thank God," she says and kisses my shoulder. "I'm so tired. But if you want to, I can probably turn over and give you access."

"You're so romantic."

She snorts and I push her onto her back and bury my face in her neck, breathing her in. "I always want you, Mia. Even when I'm bone tired from dancing the night away with you, I crave you. It wouldn't take much for me to slip inside you and lazily make love to you until we're both gasping for breath.

"But we're tired. Tonight was a fun adventure. One I'd very much like to repeat in the not-too-distant future. Not every night needs to end with mind-blowing sex. I'm content to hold you. To be with you. To just feel you against me."

"You *are* romantic," she says quietly while running her fingers through my hair. "I like it. I've never been one for romance, but when it comes from you, I like it very much."

I smile and kiss her softly, and return us to the way we were. "Go to sleep, Mia."

She clears her throat and kisses my shoulder again. "Okay. Sleep well, love."

She falls into a deep sleep, breathing evenly, and now my eyes are wide open. Maybe it was a slip of the tongue, something to say as she falls asleep. She's exhausted. Would she have used that word if she were wide awake?

I don't think so.

Yet, hearing it from her lips has ignited a fire in me that I didn't know existed. I do love Mia. Fiercely. I want to claim her, to be with her for as long as I live. My life just isn't the same when she isn't in it.

And I'm *ready* to give her the words.

To make her feel the way I feel right now. I know that she didn't say *I love you* and that she was already half asleep when she said it.

I don't care.

I need to tell her.

Chapter Thirteen

~Mia~

"How's the new guy?" Camden asks as I change lanes on the freeway west of Portland. We're on our way to my favorite orchard to pick apples.

"Pete's great," I reply with a nod.

"What do you like best about him?"

I love that Camden asks me thought-provoking questions. He doesn't just leave the conversation at *Pete's great*. He wants more.

Which tells me he pays attention *and* he gives a shit.

Basically, he's a unicorn.

"Okay, here's my list of things I like about Pete." I clear my throat. "He's super competent. Not only does he have a culinary degree, but he's worked in high-profile kitchens most of his career, so he's great under pressure."

"Very important," Camden says with a nod.

"Yes. Also, he patiently learned my recipes, and doesn't try to take liberties with them. He knows that the food sells well just the way it is and he respects that, while also suggesting new menu items to incorporate as time goes on.

"It took me *months* to develop the aphrodisiac menu, Camden. It wasn't easy. So, having someone else on hand who has ideas is refreshing."

"I can see that."

"He's tough on the other kitchen staff, but not unreasonable. I also know that he's not trying to elbow me out of my own kitchen. He's enjoying his job. And because I trust him to run the kitchen without me, I can take several days off each week to work on new recipes, or interview new vendors."

"Or spend time with your boyfriend."

I glance over to see him smiling at me, and I squeeze his hand. "Yes. Like today when he's going with me to pick apples."

"They do sell apples at most grocery stores," he says. "If not *every* grocery store."

"It's not the same as picked from the tree." I take my exit off the freeway. This orchard is about an hour from downtown Portland. It's not just an apple orchard. They also grow cherries and pears, and pumpkins for autumn.

"I can smell fall in the air."

He barks out a laugh. "That comedian was right. Women *love* fall."

"What's wrong with fall? I like pumpkins and apples and snuggling up under a blanket by a fire."

"It's still eighty degrees outside."

"It's just barely fall. I hope you've been working out because these apples aren't going to be light."

"So that's why I'm really here. For my manly muscles."

"You're the brawn in this operation," I agree as I pull into the parking lot and cut the engine. "Are you afraid of heights?"

"Not really. Why?"

"Because we will be on ladders today."

"They let customers climb ladders?"

"They don't sell pre-picked apples. This is a DIY place, and that way the apples are super fresh. They make the best pie."

He follows me into the main sales building to fetch crates for our apples, and then we set off down row after row of beautiful apple trees.

"Red or green?" he asks.

"Both." I grin and stare up at some gorgeous Granny Smith apples hanging heavily on a tree. "Look at these beauties."

"You have heart eyes, just like the emoji on my phone."

"I love apples," I reply with a shrug, and gesture for him to fetch me a free ladder from a few trees away. He drags it over to me, and I immediately climb up it to inspect the apples. "No worms that I can see."

"I should hope not."

I glance down to find him aiming his phone at me and he snaps a picture.

"Are you going to help me, or just take my picture all day?"

"Both," he says with a grin. "What do you need me to do?"

"I'm going to drop some apples down for you to put in our crates."

We take turns picking and gathering apples for about thirty minutes. When I have five crates full, he frowns up at me from the ground.

"How many pies are you planning to make?"

"Maybe ten." I shrug. "I don't know, I'll bake until the apples are finished. I'll also use the leftovers for apple butter."

"Ten? I thought you were going to make *a pie*."

"There's no sense in making just one. I'll put apple pie on the dessert menu for the next week. It's fall, so they'll sell well."

We make our way back to pay for the apples, and Camden wrestles them into my SUV, taking up the entire rear cargo space.

"This might be way too many apples, sweetheart."

"I'll find uses for them."

He laughs and gets into the car with me. "Do I get to help make the pies?"

"Of course."

"Do I get one whole pie to myself?"

"You're really selfish when it comes to pie."

"In case you forgot, it was *you* who sat in your bed and taunted me with cherry pie two weeks ago."

"Poor guy." I toss him a sassy smile and pull back onto the freeway toward home. "I'll make it up to you."

"With pie?"

"If you'd rather have pie than a blow job, yes, pie is all yours."

"You drive a hard bargain."

"You have no idea."

"THIS KITCHEN REALLY is great," he says an hour later after we've hauled all of the apples into my house. "It looks brand-new."

"It is. I mean, the renovations were finished a while ago, but I've barely used the kitchen. It was important to me that I have a chef's kitchen in my home, and that it be commercially certified so I could develop recipes and make some of the food ahead of time here at home."

"That's smart of you. Have you actually been able to do that?"

"Nope. Not even once . . . until today." I grin and preheat the oven. "So, you get to help me on my maiden voyage in the kitchen for commercial purposes."

"I'm honored." He bows deeply, then grins at me. "Where do you want me?"

"Everywhere. But for this project, we probably shouldn't have sex here. It's just not sanitary."

"You're funny," he says and reaches for a crate of apples, plopping it on my countertop. "Where do we start?"

"I'm going to fill some big bowls with cold water so we can start peeling them without them going brown." After the bowls are full I set them on my massive island, pull out two cutting boards, and offer him a knife.

"I have my knives in my car," he says. "I'll be right back."

There are perks to being with a chef. He knows the importance of keeping his own knives nearby.

No one else would get it.

He returns with what looks like a suitcase that should either have a million dollars in small, unmarked bills, or a bomb in it.

Instead, he opens it and his knives are set in black foam. They gleam in the light from my kitchen.

"Those are gorgeous."

"They're good knives. You have good ones, too."

We each get to work peeling and slicing apples; and when one bowl is full, I set it aside.

"If you don't mind, you can keep peeling and I'll start on the crusts."

He just nods and keeps working on the apples.

"Whose recipe do you use for this?"

"My mother's. I've helped her bake pies since I was a little girl."

"Is apple pie popular in Italy?"

I smile and shake my head. "When she and Daddy moved here, it was important to her that she fit in. She wanted to cook American meals. She wanted to make friends with her neighbors, and she definitely didn't want to be an outsider.

"So, she gathered recipes from her neighbors and would even go spend time in their kitchens, watching them. Apple pies are her favorite."

"Your parents are—"

"Old fashioned? A little odd? Nosy as fuck? Yeah, they're all those things. And they are wonderful parents. Landon and I were always loved and never went without much. My dad has been a contractor for as long as I can remember. He worked his ass off so Mom could stay home with us, and they made a nice life for themselves here."

"They love you very much."

I nod and add some apples to a pot to boil with sugar and cinnamon. "Sometimes they use the *we love you so much* just so they can intrude. Try to take control. Embarrass their children."

"I think most parents do that," he says with a laugh. "That's not necessarily an Italian trait."

"I know." I sigh and glance over my shoulder at him. "And I don't mean to complain, especially when I'm standing near a man who no longer has his parents. It's not that I'm ungrateful."

"I know. It gets frustrating. Do you make pies like this for the restaurant every year?"

"I usually have apple pie on the menu for fall, but I've never been able to make them ahead like this. I normally make them every day at Seduction. And we run out after being open for an hour. Even if I bake twenty pies, they'll be gone in three days."

"I'm so proud of you, Mia."

My head whips up in surprise.

"I mean it," he continues. The apples are all peeled and sliced now, and he's leaning against the countertop, his arms crossed over his chest. "What you've done with your restaurant is beyond impressive."

"It's taken a village. There are five of us," I remind him, but he shakes his head.

"I'm not trying to take anything away from the others.

It's obvious that you all live and breathe that place. But as a chef, I know how much work goes into designing a kitchen, building a menu, and all of the little things that no one else thinks about. You've put a lot of yourself into it."

"I have," I agree and stir the apples, then get to work on the crusts. "And you're right. There were plenty of nights when the girls would go home around midnight and I'd stay through the night. Especially in the beginning. I'm not telling you this for sympathy."

"I know."

"I just enjoy experimenting, and I really *love* my job."

"I know that too."

"So it's been a labor of love for all of us. The aphrodisiac element was my idea. I liked the thought of our place being sexy. A place where a newlywed couple could come, or maybe a first date. Anniversaries. People say all the time, my husband took me out on a date, and I wanted us to open a place that catered to date night.

"It's in every element of the place. Not just the food. Addie designed a wonderful dining room, with rich fabrics. Comfortable colors that relax and stir the senses. The music piped through the place is sexy. It came together better than any of us expected."

"It's a sensation," he says with a nod. "I heard about it not long after you opened. I didn't know you were one of the owners at the time, but your restaurant made its way through the food grapevine. What you've done is remarkable."

"Thank you." I smile widely and lay the crust in a pie plate, then fill it with apples. "That means a lot."

"What can I do now?"

"These two are about to go in the oven. If you want to start more apples in the pot for two more pies, we'll get them going as well."

For the next twenty minutes, we work side by side, not needing to talk at all. The quiet is comfortable, and my house is beginning to smell amazing.

"Hello?"

Landon's voice calls out from my front door just as the next two pies go into the oven. Camden and I walk out of the kitchen to greet him.

"Hey," Camden says and shakes Landon's hand. "How are you?"

"Good." Landon smiles at me and cocks a brow. "How are *you*?"

"I'm good too," I reply. He sniffs deeply.

"Pie!"

"It's still baking," I inform him, rolling my eyes.

"Great. I'll stay long enough to have hot pie." He grins and takes a seat at my dining room table.

"Is that the only reason you're here? Did your psychic powers tell you that we're baking today?"

"I don't have psychic powers," Landon informs Camden, who only smiles in response. "I just had a few hours free and thought I'd swing by to see you. Cami said you took the day off."

"I did. Camden and I went to the orchard for apples."

"So I take it the new chef is working out?"

"He's really great," I reply with a nod. "And I trust him, so I *can* take more days off."

"I'm glad. You worried me."

"Oh please." I roll my eyes and stand when I hear the timer in the kitchen. "The first two are done."

I rush back to pull them out of the oven, set them on cooling racks, and return to the dining room.

"You saying that you're worried about me is ridiculous," I say, carrying on where I left off.

"Why?" Landon asks.

"Because you used to fly fighter jets in enemy territory. *That* is worth being worried over."

"Did you really?" Camden asks.

"Mia never told you?" Landon asks. Camden shakes his head.

"No, if I remember right, she just said that her brother was in the navy."

"I was, but she left out the best part." He glares at me, and I know it's all in fun. Landon isn't one to brag. "I flew jets. I was stationed on aircraft carriers for years."

"What made you decide to get out?"

"I had an accident," he says and shakes his head. "I had to eject, and once you do that, your career is over."

"I had no idea."

Landon nods. "Most guys, if they walk away from an ejection, suffer from head or spinal injuries. But even if you don't, you can never be released to fly again. I didn't want to ride a desk, so I got out."

"How have you been feeling?" I ask him.

"I'm fit as a fiddle. And I want pie."

"It's still cooling."

"That's when it's best." He turns on his pouty face and bats his eyelashes at me, and I roll my eyes and stand. "Fine, I'll cut you some. Would you like a piece, Camden?"

"Sure. Thanks, sweetheart."

I walk back into the kitchen and cut us each a slice, then scoop out vanilla ice cream to go with it. I use my pretty dessert plates because it makes me happy.

The guys probably won't even notice.

Just as I've loaded up my tray and am about to return to the dining room, I can hear Landon speaking in a low, serious tone.

So of course I stop and listen.

"I know you care about her," Landon says. "I can see that, and from what I can see, you're a decent guy. She has it bad for you and I'm happy for her. I really am. But just be gentle with her. I don't think she's had a lot of gentle in her life, especially from men."

"I have no intentions to hurt her," Camden says, also in a hushed tone.

"I should hope not," Landon says. "I know she comes off as being really badass and tough, and trust me when I say that most of the time she is those things. But she also has one of the kindest hearts I know. Once she lets someone into her life, she doesn't half-ass it. She loves big, Camden. And if she trusts you, you'd best make damn sure you don't fuck that up; because with Mia, once the trust is gone, you're toast. She may forgive, but she never forgets."

"I know that too," Camden says. "I don't know how or why I've been given this second opportunity to have her in my life, but here it is all the same, and I am not going to fuck it up."

"Glad to hear it, man."

I have to clear my throat and will the tears to stay at bay. Two of the most important men in my life just had a come-to-Jesus conversation for me.

I think that's a first.

I've had plenty of them with other people, but I don't think that Landon or Dad have ever tried to warn off a guy I was interested in.

Not that I brought many of them around.

I walk back into the dining room and pass around the dessert. The ice cream has just barely started to melt.

"Vanilla ice cream too?" Camden asks and digs in.

"I'm no beginner. My dessert game is strong."

"It's early for dessert," Landon says with a frown, checking the clock on the wall.

"It's never too early for dessert," I reply and take a bite. "You can take the rest of this pie home to share with Cami."

"Thanks."

"And I mean *share with Cami*. She told me what happened the last time I sent that cake home with you."

"What happened?" Camden asks.

"I put it in the microwave," Landon says defensively.

"And you forgot to tell Cami that it was there."

He cringes. "So, I'd go into the kitchen and think, *Oh, there's cake.* And I'd cut myself a piece, eat it, and go about my day. That happened every day until the cake was gone."

"And then a few days later, I asked Cami if she liked the cake. And she was like, *What cake?*"

"Not a smart move, man," Camden says, laughing.

"Trust me, I've been reminded over and over to never do it again."

"Especially now that she's pregnant," I say and feel my heart soften. "I haven't seen much of you since Cami told us. How are you doing?"

"I'm nervous," he admits and turns to Camden. "We lost a baby when we first got married. We weren't sure if she could have children after that."

"But here we are," I say and reach over to squeeze his hand. "Cami's healthy, and that's going to be one spoiled little baby."

"Yeah." He grins and takes another bite of pie. "And if I forget to tell her that we have pie, she'll cut my dick off."

"That seems harsh," Camden says.

"Well, I put the toilet paper on the roll backwards, and she threatened my manhood over that, and this would be much worse."

"Maybe I should send her a pie just for her."

"Not a bad idea," Landon says.

Chapter Fourteen

~Camden~

*H*ey Camden," Addie says in greeting when I walk through the front door of Seduction two weeks later.

"Hi. Is Mia in the kitchen?"

"She is." She bites her lip and looks back toward Mia's domain. "You may not want to go back there."

"Why? Is she okay?"

"Oh, she's fine." Addie nods, but her face has uncertainty written all over it. "But she's in a mood."

"I brought coffee," I reply confidently, and saunter through the dining room to the kitchen. I open the door and stop dead, taking in the scene before me.

There are two sous chefs on staff today, and they're both scurrying around as if they've just had a fire lit under them.

Mia is nowhere to be seen.

"Excuse me."

No one looks up from their task, and Mia hurries out of the walk-in freezer.

"Hi," I say and walk over to her. I hold the coffee out, suddenly very unsure of myself.

"Hello yourself," she says.

"I brought coffee."

"Thank you." She offers me a quick smile then gestures to the countertop beside her. "You can set it down."

She hurries away again, but before I can turn around, she's back.

"Do you need something, Camden?" she asks. She's clearly busy, and maybe a bit pissed off, so I do what I know to do with Mia.

I wrap my arms around her from behind and hug her. She stiffens. "I'm at work."

"So you are."

"Seriously, Camden." She wiggles away and turns to face me now, no humor anywhere on her face. "What's up?"

"I was just thinking about you, so I thought I'd stop in and bring you something. See if I can help out."

"I don't need any help today," she says and turns away. "Thanks for the coffee."

"It's gonna get cold if you don't drink it."

She stops what she's doing, sighs, picks up the cup, and takes a sip.

"Yum. Thanks."

"You're welcome." I smile brightly, but she doesn't return it. "What's going on, Mia?"

"I'm just trying to catch up here. These two yayhoos were

supposed to come in early today to prep for later, and neither of them *remembered*." She says *remembered* with finger quotation marks. "So here we are, busting ass to be ready on time."

"I told you, I can help."

"I don't *need* your help. I need the people I pay good money to to show up on fucking time." She glares at the others. Neither is brave enough to look up. "So, thanks for the coffee, but I don't have time to stand here and entertain you."

"Must be about to start her period," I mumble and turn away. I don't reach the door before I hear one of the sous chefs say, "Dumbass."

"What did you just say?" Mia demands. I turn around to find her standing with her hands fisted on her hips and her blue eyes shooting fire.

She's gorgeous when she's pissed off.

"I was just making an observation," I reply. "You weren't this moody this morning, which was literally two hours ago. And now I can't seem to do anything right."

"God grant me the strength to not beat the shit out of the people around me today," she says as she scrubs her hands over her face. "You know what, Camden, I'll see you tomorrow. I can't *even* deal with you right now. Or later."

"I can meet you at your place—"

"*Tomorrow*," she repeats, eyes narrowed.

"Fine."

I turn and march out of the kitchen, but rather than leave, I walk into the bar. Kat's behind it, rotating liquor bottles.

"Hey Camden, what can I do for you?" she asks with a

smile. I don't know Kat well, but from what I've seen of her, I like her. She has a style all of her own, with her flaming red hair and interesting outfits. Today she's in a red shirt with white polka dots. It's tied at her waist, and she's wearing short denim shorts.

It works for her.

"Hi, Kat." I sit on a stool and sigh. "I need a drink."

"It's not even noon yet."

"And yet, here I am. Don't make me beg."

She smirks. "What's your poison?"

"Whiskey. Neat."

"Wow." She pulls a glass down and pours two fingers of whiskey in it, then slides it over.

I swallow it, then pass it back for more.

This time, when she hands it back to me, I sip it.

"So, are you going to tell me why you're drinking straight whiskey this early in the day?"

"Maybe I just like to drink a lot."

"*Do* you like to drink a lot?"

"No."

"Well, then." She smiles and sets her work aside so she can listen to me. "What's up?"

"You seem oddly easy to talk to."

"I have a psychology degree."

"Should I call you Doc?"

"Nah. Just Kat."

I nod and sip my drink. "Mia's pissed at me."

"Yeah, I heard she was on a tear this morning. That hasn't happened in a while. Since you got here, actually."

"I have no idea why she's pissed."

"It probably has nothing at all to do with you," she says reasonably.

"Then why is she taking it out on me?"

"Because you're the person who means the most to her. Of course she's going to take it out on you. How old are you, Camden?"

"Thirty-two."

"And you're just now finding out that women can take out their frustration and anger on you even if it's not your fault? I would think this is something you'd have experience in far sooner than this."

"I don't think I really cared before," I answer truthfully. "Most of my previous relationships have been casual. I work a lot of hours. I don't have time to invest in a relationship."

"I hope you're about to say *until now*."

"Until now," I reply with a smile and sip my whiskey. "She has quite the temper."

"Oh, this is nothing. She's a pussycat this morning." Kat laughs and takes a drink of her own coffee. Suddenly, I can hear Mia yelling, but I can't make out the words. "Okay, now it's moved into pissed off territory."

"She said her help didn't come in on time this morning."

"That'll do it," Kat says with a nod. "She works her ass off, and she expects the help to work just as hard. Which, unfortunately, isn't likely. They don't own this place. Their success doesn't hang in the balance of whether or not we succeed. If we don't, they move on to another restaurant. But the rest of us will be fucked."

"I hear you," I reply with a nod. "She's talked to me about the lack of work ethic in the people she's hired before. It's got to be disappointing."

"For sure. I had another bartender quit on me yesterday and that's the third one since summer started." She shrugs. "I'd love to take a weekend away with my husband, but I can't just go. I know the girls would cover for me. Riley's not a half-bad bartender when she has to be. But, this is *my* responsibility. I know Mia feels the same way."

I nod and swallow down the last of my drink. "Thanks."

"You're welcome. I hope you don't plan to drive home now."

"I'm gonna go find a place to have breakfast, on foot, and then I'll head home. I'm fine, though, Kat."

"I trust that you are," she says. "I hope your day gets better."

"I've been cut off until tomorrow," I inform her. "So, it's going to pretty much suck. I know we haven't been seeing each other for long, but I miss her when she isn't around."

"That's sweet." Kat smiles. "And I know what you mean. I miss Mac too. Maybe if you call her later, you can talk her into letting you come over."

"I think I'll give her some space." I stand. "What do I owe you?"

"This one's on the house." She winks at me and I nod, then leave the bar and pass by Addie on my way out.

"How did it go?" Addie asks.

"Well, we're lucky that I don't need an ambulance for stab wounds."

She covers her mouth with her hand, trying to cover her laughter. "Well, there's that, I guess."

"Yeah."

"To be fair, I did try to warn you."

"You did. It was my fault. Next time, I'll leave the coffee with you and make a hasty retreat."

"Good idea."

Twenty-four hours without her and I want to punch something.

Or someone.

I texted her this morning, but didn't get a response, so I'll just see if she's home. I miss her. And I'll be damned if she's going to shut me out now.

Her car is in her driveway. Taking that as a good sign, I knock on the front door, but there's no answer. It's unlocked, so I walk in and listen.

It's quiet. Maybe she's sleeping.

"Mia?" I call out and leave my phone, wallet, and keys by the front door. There's no answer as I walk through the living space and check her bedroom. The covers are messy, but she's not in her bed.

Not in the shower.

I backtrack to the kitchen, but she's not here either. The back door is open, and I can see her kneeling in the garden. I lean on the doorjamb and watch her for a long moment.

Her long curly hair is tied back in a tail, and she's wearing a pink, wide-brimmed hat to hide her face from the sun.

She's wearing gardening gloves, and is ripping weeds out of the earth as if they've all personally offended her.

I walk down the steps and stop next to her. She glances my way, but doesn't even pause.

"Good morning," I say and shove my hands in my pockets.

"Hello."

She still doesn't look up at me, so I decide to enjoy the quiet and just work next to her for a while. Her wheelbarrow is across the yard, so I fetch it and load it with the weeds she's already pulled, then I start at the opposite side of the garden from her and begin to pull weeds myself. When I'm about ten feet from her, I gather my weeds and toss them in the wheelbarrow.

"How are you today, Mia?"

"I'm pretty good," she says quietly.

"You know, I realize that I owe you an apology for something I said yesterday, but I'm not entirely sure what that is. What did I say?"

She finally sits back on her haunches, pushes her hat high on her forehead, and looks up at me. She's wearing sunglasses, but she takes them off, and I'm glad to be able to see her blue eyes, which are a bit shiny, as if she was crying earlier.

"I know that it's considered funny by men to accuse a woman of being on her period if she's in a bad mood. I get it. But frankly, I don't think it's funny." She stands and takes her gloves off, slapping them against her leg to knock the excess dirt off. "In fact, I think it's a passive aggressive way of calling me a bitch. So, you called me a bitch."

"That's not at all what I meant."

"Doesn't matter," she says with a shrug. "I heard a really good quote once that went something like, 'When a person tells you that you've hurt them, you don't get to decide that you didn't.'"

"I would *never* intentionally hurt you, Mia."

She nods once, glances down at her gloves and then sighs. "I know that I can fly off the handle, and most of the time, I'm told that I'm being irrational. But between the morning I had before you came in, and then hearing you call me a bitch, it was the perfect storm for me to be pissy. And I'll apologize for taking it out on you, because that was my fault, and it wasn't fair."

She swallows hard and bends over to pull one weed that she missed.

"I'm sorry that I didn't realize how upset you were," I reply and reach out to brush some dirt from her cheek.

"I overreact," she says, but I shake my head in disagreement.

"You're passionate," I reply. "I don't think you overreact at all. You feel your emotions deeply, and you express them passionately. You're not trying to be a drama queen."

She's watching me now with wide eyes. "You know, I've never thought of it that way before."

"It's true." I pull her in for a hug, and feel the weight of the past twenty-four hours lift from my shoulders. "What else can I help with?"

"Well, if you don't mind watering the plants with the hose over there, I'll start picking some of the veggies. I haven't done that yet, I was too busy weeding."

"I can do that." I kiss her forehead and hold her chin in my fingers. "Are we okay?"

"Yeah." She grins. "Thanks for coming over."

"I tried to text you but I didn't get a response."

"I turned my phone off last night and haven't looked at it since. I need some time to just *be*. I'm sorry if you were worried."

"I'm okay." I turn on the hose and drag it over to the garden, and begin to water the plants. The nozzle on the hose lets just a trickle of water out, so although it takes longer to water, it doesn't harm the plants.

"Look at these carrots," she says with excitement, holding up some impressively big carrots. "These are going to be perfect in the salads."

We work side by side for a while. When her bounty is all collected, she takes it inside, then returns to help clean up. She's just dumped the weeds out of the wheelbarrow, and turned back toward me when I decide to point the hose at her and turn the spray up.

"Oh my God!" she cries and holds her hands up over her face. "What the fuck?"

She's laughing, so I spray her again. She runs to the opposite side of the house, and before I know it, she returns with another hose turned on full blast.

"Two can play this game, buddy."

She sprays me, and then turns her back to me so my spray hits her shoulders.

"It's so cold!"

We run all over the backyard getting each other and everything else sopping wet.

"Uncle," she cries and drops her hose, holding her hands up in surrender. "I can't." She's laughing so hard, she can hardly catch her breath. "Seriously."

I drop my hose too and tackle her to the ground, roll us until she's under me, and drag hair that worked its way out of the ponytail off of her face.

"I love you, Mia."

She immediately stops laughing and stares up at me. "Wait. What?"

"You heard me." I kiss her cheek and then her forehead. "Why do you look so surprised?"

"I don't know." She leans away so she can look in my eyes. "Maybe because you've never said it before."

"I've been wanting to say it for a long time," I admit with a shrug and then kiss her sweet lips. I should have told her weeks ago, but I didn't want the moment to seem forced. "Playing with you, watching you laugh, is one of my favorite things with you, and I just couldn't help myself."

"I look horrible," she says. "I'm in my grimiest clothes, my hair is a wreck, I probably have dirt in all of my most secret places."

"You didn't bathe in the garden, did you, sweetheart?"

She grins. "No."

"So probably just dirty on the outside, then." I rub a particularly dirty patch on her cheek. "But still gorgeous, and I'm still in love with you."

She closes her eyes, and looks like she's physically having a hard time letting the words soak in.

"Look at me. Why don't you believe me?"

"I didn't say that I don't believe you," she says, but still won't look me in the eye. She's toying with a string on the sleeve of my T-shirt. "I don't think you're lying."

"Well, that's good to know," I reply, but still can't figure out the lack of response from her. "Mia?"

"Uh huh."

I kiss her deeply, plant my thigh between her legs, and feel her immediate arousal. She's clinging to me, but she ends the kiss and stares in my eyes for a moment, until I ask, "What is it?"

"Why?"

"Why what?"

"Why do you love me?"

I pause, thrown by the question. Jesus, there are a billion reasons to love this woman, I have no idea how to go about listing them. But the most important question of all is, *why* does she need to ask me that?

"Don't you think you're loveable?"

She frowns—and a myriad of emotions play over her face before she looks away—and I can see tears threatening to form. The last thing in the world that I ever want to see is Mia in tears; so before she can answer me, I stand up and hold my hand out to help her up off the ground, which she immediately takes.

I lead her into the house, through the kitchen and into the living room where I dropped my phone.

"I want to show you something."

Chapter Fifteen

~Mia~

*H*oly fuck.

He's staring down at me with so much raw emotion in his face, in his voice, that I don't even know what to do.

Do I say it back to him? Because I want to more than anything. I love him so much that my chest aches with it.

"Don't you think you're loveable?" he asks and drags his fingertips down my cheek.

I don't know.

That's the ridiculous response that's running through my head. I don't know if I'm loveable. Or worthy of love, at least from him. The girls all love me, and my family loves me, but this is *so different*.

Suddenly he stands and helps me to my feet, then leads me into the house. I'm not even going to think about the fact that we're tracking dirt and water through the house that I spent all morning cleaning. He grabs his phone and turns back to me.

"I want to show you something."

He pulls me onto the couch next to him, cuddles me, and wakes up his phone from standby so I can see the screen. He opens his photos, then finds a folder that's labeled *Mia*.

"This photo," he begins as he starts at the most recent image, "was the other day when we were watching that horror movie. You were curled up in the corner of the couch, that orange blanket pulled up to your chin, and your eyes were so damn wide. I love your blue eyes, by the way."

He scrolls to the next photo. "This was at the farmer's market this week. You were smelling the peaches, and the look of pure joy on your face is just stunning. I love how much you love food. Oh, and this one was that morning that you slept through your alarm."

"I'm sleeping in this photo."

"Yes, *I* woke up with the alarm, and I knew I needed to capture this. Look at how sweet you look!"

I would call it a hot mess, but I'm not going to argue.

He flips through a few more photos, then stops on one where I'm laughing.

"Is this at that comedy show?" I ask.

"Yep, and I love it when you laugh."

"I look horrible in this one. I have about fourteen chins."

"No you don't," he says and kisses my forehead. "Besides, you're making my favorite sound in this picture."

"Did I snort?"

"No, you're giggling."

"My giggle is your favorite sound?"

"It is," he says and shows me a photo he took while we were dancing. "Look at how happy you are here. You seriously *love* to dance."

"Yeah." I grin and examine this photo. I was wearing the cute black top that Addie helped me pick out, along with some skinny jeans and fun shoes. "I felt sexy that night."

"You were so fucking sexy that night that I thought I was going to have to kill some of the fuckers who kept eyeballing you."

"Whatever," I reply with a snort, but he looks down at me with deadly serious eyes.

"Trust me, they were looking."

"But I only have eyes for you," I reply and bat my eyelashes.

He kisses me and flips to the next photo.

He flips to one of me just smiling at him from the top of a ladder at the orchard. "That was a fun day."

"The pies went over amazingly at the restaurant," I reply with a nod. "And yeah, the whole day was fun. Picking the apples and making the pies together. I enjoy being with you."

He smiles down at me and keeps going through the photos.

"This was during filming," he continues, and shows me a photo with my back to him, and my hip is cocked to the side. "Did you know that you dance while you cook?"

"Yeah, I catch myself doing that a lot. I try not to do it in front of the others at work."

"I fucking love it when you do that," he says with a smile. "It's like you have your two favorite things at the same time: food and dancing."

"Cooking makes me happy, so I dance."

"It's sexy as all get-out, so don't stop doing it on my behalf," he says. He shows me a few more, and then flips to a photo that makes me stop cold.

"Camden."

"This was the day before you left me." His voice is quieter now. "We'd been married for about two days, and you had made us dinner. You said—"

"I wanted to cook something delicious for my husband," I whisper and clench my eyes closed. I'm so young in that picture. "I'm a horrible person."

"You, you aren't. Keep looking. Here's one from the day you told me you thought you were pregnant."

"I look terrified."

He nods. "I haven't looked at this photo in a long time. You're right, you do look terrified."

We're quiet for a moment, and then he flips to more of me laughing, sticking my tongue out at him, while dressed in my school uniform and holding a measuring cup full of milk.

"I was so young," I murmur. "And thinner."

"We were all thinner then," he says with a smile.

"Oh please. If you've gained a pound at all it's just because you're even more muscly than before." I squeeze his bicep and he obliges me with a flex, making me grin. "I really do appreciate your arms."

"Good to know," he says, wiggling his eyebrows. "This is the last photo."

It's just me. Sitting at my desk in school, smiling shyly at him.

"This was before we moved in together."

He nods and sets his phone aside. "I've loved you for a very long time, Mia."

I swallow hard, honestly surprised. "Why didn't you ever tell me?"

He sighs. "I wanted to. I'm just not good at saying the words. I think that if I *show* you—by doing nice things for you, holding you, being affectionate—that I don't need to say the words."

"Why is it hard for you to say it? Did you have a crappy childhood or something?"

He shakes his head. "Not at all. I had a great childhood. I'm no shrink, but it's probably because of the way my parents died when I was a teenager."

"You never speak of them."

"I know, and that's not right because they were awesome parents, Mia. Steph is four years older than me. I was sixteen, and she was away at college when it happened."

I want to ask him a million questions, but I sit and wait patiently as he gathers his thoughts.

"They had gone to New York on a business trip for Dad, and they were in the car on the way to the airport. They'd called me to make sure that I had cleaned the house. Mom hated coming home to a dirty house. Steph was in college, but she went close to home, so she'd been staying there with me while they were gone.

"She spoke to them and then handed the phone to me. My mom sounded happy, and she was ready to go home. They'd only been gone for about a week. We were joking about something, and she said, '*I love you, kiddo.*' I said, '*I love you too.*' And as soon as I said that, I heard an enormous crash. They'd been hit by a semi on the freeway. He wasn't looking and he hit them head-on."

"Oh, Camden." I kiss his hand gently. "You were on the phone with them when it happened?"

"Yeah. And it was the last thing I said to her."

"That's a gift," I reply. "So many people wish they'd been able to tell their loved ones that they loved them before they passed."

"I know. I don't have that regret." He smiles sadly. "But it was probably the worst moment in my life, only above the day I came home to find you gone. I don't say that to make you feel guilty all over again, Mia.

"I was a typical kid. Saying *I love you* wasn't really in my vocabulary much anyway, and then they passed away. Steph was my guardian, and probably the most patient person on the world, after that. I had a rough year. I was angry."

"Of course you were."

"But I just don't want any more time to slip by without telling you how I feel. I've wanted to say it for weeks now, and it's stupid that I was waiting until the *right* moment. I should just tell you."

"Thank you."

Oh good Lord, girl, he says he loves you and you say thank you?

"Are you cold?" he asks.

"Yeah, we should probably get out of these wet clothes."

"Did we ruin your couch?"

"I doubt it." I stand and help him to his feet this time. "Let's have a shower."

We shed out of our clothes, and I start the water in the shower. I expect him to attack me, to boost me up against the wall and fuck me brainless, but he doesn't.

Instead, he urges me to get my hair wet, then pours some shampoo in his hands and lathers it into my hair, scrubbing my scalp.

"Oh, dear God, that feels good."

He's slow and thorough, and when he's lathered it up really well, he helps me rinse it and does the same with conditioner.

While that sits in my hair, he pumps my body wash in his hands and slowly lathers it all over my body, paying particular attention to my breasts.

"Are they dirty?" I ask innocently.

"Very." He swirls the soap around each one, making my nipples pucker, then travels down to my navel. He makes a heart in the soap, my navel in the middle of it, then travels lower. "Brace your leg on the bench."

"Yes, sir." I comply and then have to bite my lip when his hand dives between my legs, gently washing and massaging me in the most intimate way possible. "Camden."

"Yes, love."

I gasp, unable to speak anymore, and lean in to bite his shoulder.

"Have I told you that it makes me crazy when you bite me?"

I shake my head no and cry out when he presses on my clit.

"Everything you do turns me on," he growls against my ear. His hands leave my core and he washes my inner thighs, my legs, and squats next to me to wash my feet. "Stand under the spray."

I love it when he gets bossy. He rinses the suds off my body, and then I tip my head back into the water so the conditioner can rinse out of my hair.

When I'm thoroughly clean, he moves to turn the water off, but I stop him.

"Oh no. It's your turn."

He cocks a brow, but he obeys when I tell him to trade places. The water splashes onto him, getting him wet. I can't reach his hair well to wash it, so after he gets it wet, he bends over. I lather his hair, loving the way the thick strands feel between my fingers.

"You have great hair."

He just grunts and I reach for the removable water wand to rinse his hair. I reach for the conditioner, but he shakes his head no.

So I pump the body wash into my hands and lather them up, then get to work on his ridiculously sexy body. His dick is standing at attention, but I don't touch it yet. I concentrate on his shoulders, his stomach, and his legs; and once he's rinsed off, I start over again with the body wash. But this time I kneel before him, and smile up at him as I wrap my sudsy hands around his cock and massage it.

"Fuck." He closes his eyes and leans his hands against the shower wall as I pleasure him, loving how hard he is— how the vein on the underside of his cock is full and stands out. I rinse him off and lean in to suck it, but he grabs me by the shoulders and lifts me to my feet. "Not now."

"You made *me* come," I argue, but he just shakes his head.

"I want to be inside of you," he says. "But not yet."

"Do we *always* have to take it slow?"

He grins. "No. We're not going to take this slow. But we're not going to do it here."

He cuts the water off and wraps me in a towel, then wipes me mostly dry, takes my hand, and leads me to my bed.

The next thing I know, I'm on my back, my legs have been pushed up and he's eating me out like a man starved.

My hands immediately clench in his hair, keeping him pressed to me. I arch my back as I come spectacularly, every hair on my body standing on end.

"Camden."

"Hmm." He's not stopping, despite my already coming. His tongue is inside me, and he presses his thumb to my clit again, making me come again.

I might die.

I'm dead.

My arms and legs feel numb. I feel exhausted, but he climbs over me, cups my cheek in his hand and kisses me deeply. I can taste myself, and that seems to reawaken me.

"I want you," I murmur against his lips. "Right now."

He slides inside me, but then pulls right back out and mutters, "Shit. Condom." He's gone for a split second, and then he's inside me, braced over me, and buried so deep inside of me I don't know where I end and he begins.

I can't stop watching his face. He looks stern and turned on, and happy all at once. I didn't even know that was possible.

"Mine," he says and presses his forehead to mine, moving his nose back and forth. "You are mine, Mia. Do you understand me?"

"Yes." I smile and wrap my legs around his waist, urging him deeper. "I'm yours, Camden."

He sighs and closes his eyes just as I feel every muscle in his body tense. He stops moving, pulls out and flips me over. He grips onto my hips and plunges inside me again, fucking me hard now, the only sound in the room is the slapping of skin, and the moans of pleasure. I look up into the mirror by my bed, and Camden grins at me.

"Do you see how fucking sexy you are?"

"We're sexy," I reply and reach down to cup his balls. "*We* are sexy."

His eyes close, and he comes apart, pushing and grinding against me, riding the wave of his own orgasm.

His teeth are clenched, he's drenched in sweat. My ass

is in the air, pressed against him, and I don't think I've ever seen anything sexier in my life.

He finally pulls out and I collapse onto the bed in exhaustion. I hear the toilet flush, and he joins me, pulls the covers up over us.

"We need to change these sheets," I murmur.

"Seems we're making all kinds of messes today," he says with a laugh. "I'll clean it all up."

"I can help." I yawn and trace his collarbones. "I love you too, you know. I loved you back then, and I love you all over again."

He turns me onto my back and hovers over me, watching me closely.

"I didn't say it because I was afraid that you didn't feel the same way. I was afraid that you'd say it back out of pity, or even worse, you wouldn't say anything at all and I'd be mortified. Sometimes I can read your mood, but I'm not a mind reader. I didn't know, Camden."

"I know."

"I tried to forget you. I tried to move on with my life and forget that I ever loved you so much that it hurt to breathe." I swallow hard and lick my lips. "And I did. For a while. But the minute I saw you again, I knew that I'd never really gotten over you."

"I'm here now," he says. "We've screwed things up in the past, but I'm here now, Mia, and I don't plan on going anywhere. Jesus, I moved to Portland *for you*."

"You're still living in a rental," I reply. "That has to be expensive."

"Only about three hundred a day."

"What?" I sit up and stare down at him in horror. "Why didn't you say so?"

"Why *would* I say so?"

"That's a shit ton of money. It's ridiculous to spend that much."

"Sweetheart, I'm loaded." He has a cocky grin on his face now. "I can afford the rental."

"You should just move in here."

"I'm not going to move in here just because you think I'm paying too much for the rental. It's not a big deal. I'll work out more permanent living conditions sooner or later. I'm not worried about it."

"I don't like it." I frown and lie back down, but I don't snuggle up to him. "It seems silly for you to be renting a place when I have this place. We've lived together before. We're not bad at it."

"You want to be roommates?" He's frowning, and I can't help but try to keep my face serious, just to play with him.

"I do have the spare bedroom. You're welcome to it. Besides, I have a better kitchen."

"You want me to be your fucking roommate." It's not a question.

"I won't charge you anything for rent, since I have to make the mortgage anyway, but if you could help out with utilities, that would be fantastic."

He laughs now and shakes his head. "You better be fucking with me, baby."

"Or?"

He pulls me to him and kisses me hard, then pulls away when we're both breathing hard. "What do you want, Mia?"

"I want you here."

"Okay then. See? That wasn't so hard."

I bark out a laugh. "Everything's been hard with you, Camden."

Chapter Sixteen

~Camden~

*Y*ou have a beautiful home," Mia says to my sister three weeks later as we sit outside in the backyard. We came up to Seattle to see Steph and Chip, and to just get out of Portland for twenty-four hours.

"Thank you," Steph says with a smile. "Camden says yours is beautiful too."

"It's finally getting there," Mia replies. "I've had some renovations done since I bought the place. It's pretty much where I want it now."

"I moved in there this week," I add and grin when Steph's gaze swings quickly to mine, her eyes wide.

"Really?"

"Really."

"It didn't make sense for him to keep renting the house

he was in," Mia says, but then grins at me. "And, I like it better having him with me. He's not a bad roommate."

"He's bad at laundry," Steph warns Mia, who just laughs.

"I'm good at laundry, so we're okay. He has other talents."

"I can do this thing with my tongue—"

"Ew!" Steph covers her ears with her hands and squeezes her eyes shut. "Stop talking. That's enough."

"Don't you know that your sister still thinks you're a virgin?" Chip asks as he joins us on the patio, carrying a platter of steaks. "These beauties are ready to go on the grill."

"I'll help." I stand, but he shoos me back.

"I've got this. I'm right here." He opens the grill and smiles at Steph. "Your sister got me this very manly grill for my birthday."

"It's top of the line," Steph says proudly. "He's wanted a new one for a while."

"There's a bit of pressure, cooking for two celebrity chefs," he says, and wipes pretend sweat from his brow. "At least I know if things start to get tricky, you guys can save me."

"You're great at the grill," I reply, shaking my head. I've always liked Chip. He's completely in love with my sister, and treats her very well.

"How's the restaurant?" Steph asks Mia, who lights up at the mention of her favorite place.

"It's doing very well," she says. "We're kicking around the idea of opening up places in Seattle and San Francisco."

"Really?" I frown. "You haven't mentioned it."

"It's still the early stages," she says with a shrug. "And frankly, I have enough on my plate with the restaurant we already have and the new show. So there's no rush, but it's good to know that it could happen."

"It's so exciting," Steph replies. "I loved it when we were there. It's such a beautiful space, and the food was *amazing*."

"Thank you," Mia says with a wide smile. "That means a lot. I've recently hired a new executive chef to help me, along with a couple of new sous chefs. Camden reminded me that being a control freak is going to put me in an early grave, so I'm learning to delegate."

Steph glances over at me. "Did you admit that you also tend to be a control freak?"

"There's no need to tell her lies," I reply, making both Chip and Steph laugh.

"He works more hours than anyone I've ever met," Chip says. His back is to us as he grills the steaks.

"I've backed off some," I remind them. "And the show is going very well. We're almost finished filming the first season."

"Oh, that's so great," Steph replies. "It's wonderful that it worked into you doing a whole show together. I'm sure you work well together."

"He's fun to work with," Mia admits, smiling at me. "He's helpful, and flirty, and makes me feel at ease in front of the camera, which isn't my normal. I get nervous."

"I watched the special they ran on Seduction. I never would have thought that you were nervous. You looked beautiful."

"Well, thanks," Mia replies. "But it's so not what I'm used to. I'd rather just be back in the kitchen, doing my thing."

"You're good at both," I reply, and watch as she squirms a bit in her seat. "And I'm not just saying that because I love you."

"I love you too," she says happily.

"Wait." Steph looks back and forth between us. "Did you hear that, Chuck?"

"I did," Chip replies. He's also spun around and is staring at me in shock.

"I thought his name was Chip," Mia whispers to me.

"His name is Charles, and I switch it up sometimes," Steph replies, then shakes her head. "But back it up. You just said that you love her."

"I do."

"Wow." She blinks at me for a moment, then smiles at Mia. "He never says that. Like, ever."

"Whatever," I reply, rolling my eyes, but she just shakes her head.

"We've talked about his. Really. He doesn't say *I love you* easily."

"I know," Mia says and reaches over to take my hand.

"That's really sweet," Steph says and looks up at Chip, who leans down and kisses her cheek.

"Don't get all emotional," Chip says and turns back to the steaks. "This is a good thing."

"It's a really good thing," she says and clears her throat. "Camden, can you please help me in the kitchen? I want to bring out the rest of dinner."

"Or, you want to talk about Mia behind her back," I reply, but stand to follow her inside. She slaps my arm, harder than usual.

"Stop it," she says. "I am not going to talk about Mia behind her back."

"It's okay," Mia says, laughing. "I'd do the same thing with my brother."

I wink at her as I walk past, and as soon as we're in her kitchen with the door closed, Steph wraps her arms around me and hugs me tightly. "I'm so happy that you're in love and that you're actually *telling* her that you love her."

"Thanks." I pat her back. "This is an extreme reaction to this, you know."

"No, it's not. I'm your big sister, and I raised your cranky teenage ass, so I get to have this moment with you. You've waited a long time to have this in your life, and I'm just so fucking happy for you."

"Thank you." I stand patiently and let her hug it out, and when she steps back, I brush a tear off her face. "Are you okay?"

"Oh yeah," she says and wipes her eyes. "I wasn't expecting to hear you say it, almost casually like that."

"I've had a week to get used to it," I reply.

"You've been saying it to each other for a whole week?"

I nod.

"And you didn't tell me?"

"What did you want me to do? Call you as soon as I said it to her to fill you in?"

"A text would have been sufficient," she says with a sniff. "I need to know these things."

"And now you know. What do we need to take outside?"

She loads me up with a platter of baked potatoes and a

big bowl of salad, and once she has all of the condiments, we make our way back outside to set the table.

"Two steaks are done," Chip says. "Who ordered medium rare?"

Mia and I both raise our hands.

"I can't eat blood," Steph says, wrinkling her nose. "Chip and I are medium-well people."

"Everyone is different," Mia says and takes a seat next to me. "Did she gush over you?"

"Yeah. It was embarrassing."

"There, there," Mia says, patting my back. "She loves you."

I nod and get to work dressing my baked potato. "I know."

Dinner is delicious, and we end up spending most of the evening out on the patio, enjoying the cool evening and conversation. It's late by the time we head back to the hotel.

"We could have driven back to Portland tonight," Mia says once we're in the hotel room. "It's not a bad drive."

"There's no need to rush," I reply, and sit next to her on the sofa in the sitting area of our suite. "What did you think?"

"I think your sister and Chip are super-nice people. Dinner was good. I'm glad we came." She smiles at me. "What did you think?"

"That I shared you for long enough with others tonight," I reply, and hug her close to me. "I'm glad you enjoyed it. They're important to me."

"I get it," she says with a sigh. "I have a tight family, too. I'm so sleepy."

"Go ahead and sleep, sweetheart." I kiss her head and

feel her getting heavier against me as she gets more tired. "I'll carry you to bed."

"I don't want to break you." I frown. I know that she doesn't mean to talk badly about herself, but I don't like it when she implies that she's too big. She's not. She's beautiful.

I'll spend tomorrow morning showing her just how amazing I think she is.

"ARE YOU READY to head home?" I ask her the following morning after checking out of the hotel.

"No." She smiles over at me and shrugs. "I thought I was last night, but I'm not. I'd like to spend some time with just you. Let's do something spontaneous."

"Like, fly to Paris?" I ask and she immediately laughs.

"Not that spontaneous. I haven't been over to the coast in years."

"Then the coast is where we will go." I wiggle my eyebrows and reach for my phone. We're sitting in my car, but haven't driven off yet. I Google *luxurious hotels on the Oregon coast* and call the first listing. Once arrangements are made I grin at Mia. "We have an ocean-view room waiting for us."

"That was easy." She settles back against the leather seat and turns on the seat warmer. "I could get used to having you handy to take care of things for me."

"Good." I take her hand in mine and kiss her knuckles. "I like doing things for you."

The drive to Cannon Beach takes a few hours, not including the extra half hour we took to swing by Mia's to grab fresh clothing on our way through Portland. By the time we arrive, it's time to check in to the hotel, and we are *not* disappointed.

"They labeled this correctly," Mia says. "It's definitely luxurious."

It's a beautiful boutique hotel right on the ocean with steps down to the sand. The big Haystack Rock is just a couple hundred yards down the beach. It's a nice afternoon. It never gets too hot here, and the sun is tucked behind billowy clouds, making it perfect for beach walking.

"Let's check-in and then head down to the beach," Mia says, mirroring my thoughts.

The check in process is quick. I'm pleased to see that they offer milk, coffee, and cookies twenty-four hours a day; and a gourmet breakfast is included in the morning. Our room is spacious, with a balcony that we can sit on and watch the sunset tonight.

"This is swanky," Mia says from inside the bathroom. "The tub is bigger than my entire bathroom at home."

"We'll take a dip in it later," I reply and step out onto the deck. With lounge chairs built for two, I can see us sitting out here and never wanting to go home.

"I love the sound of the ocean," Mia says as she joins me. She takes a deep breath and rests her head on my bicep. "It's just so beautiful."

"Are you ready to go for a walk?"

"Absolutely. I'm leaving my shoes here." She kicks out of her sandals, and we walk around the building and onto the vast beach below. The water is grey-blue and frothy white with waves. "It's not calm today."

"No. It's lovely."

She smiles up at me, takes my hand, and leads me down to the water line, where our feet can get wet as we walk toward Haystack Rock.

"This is a nice surprise. Do you do things like this often?" I ask.

"Not nearly as often as I would like," she admits. "My family used to own a cabin out here, but we used it less and less so my parents sold it about five years ago. Real estate here is crazy, so they made a nice profit on it."

"Would you like to have another place here again one day?"

She frowns, considering it. "Maybe. This is my favorite beach on the Oregon coast. I mean, look at this view."

"It's stunning."

She glances up to find me looking at her, and blushes. "I meant the ocean, not me."

"I know what you meant."

"You say some sweet things."

"I mean them," I reply. "You know how I feel about you."

"It's kind of crazy, isn't it?"

"How do you mean?"

"I don't know, I was just thinking on our way here that it's funny how fate works. Or destiny, or whatever you want to call it. Chance. Karma." She steps around a crab trying to walk its way back to the ocean. "I don't mean to keep bringing up our past. It's *in* the past, and there's no need to live there. We aren't the same people, and we're in a great place now."

"Agreed."

"I guess I just have one more question, and then I'm going to stop talking about it."

"What do you want to know, Mia?"

She stops walking and looks out at the ocean for a long moment. The wind is blowing like crazy, and she tucks her hair behind her ear. "I came here. To the cabin."

"After you left?"

She nods. "I stopped at my parents' house and asked them for the keys. They looked worried, but my dad talked Mom into giving me the keys and just letting me be. They knew I was healthy, and that I'd be safe at the cabin. They asked for an explanation when I got home, but I just gave them the barest details.

"I came here, and I walked this beach, and I thought about what I'd done. The way I'd left. I was convinced that it was the right thing to do, even though I know now that it wasn't."

"We've already talked about that," I reply.

"I know." She turns to me now. "But I never asked you why you didn't come to find me. After you saw that I was gone, why didn't you come after me?"

I sigh and push my fingers through my hair. "Do you remember what you wrote in that letter?"

She frowns. "I said that you were free to find someone you really loved."

"You said that *we* could find someone we truly loved to spend our lives with." I drag my fingertips down her cheek.

"I don't know if you worded it that way on purpose, as a bit of a dig, but it stung. So, I guess the answer is, the same reason that you left—thinking that you didn't love me and we weren't in a *real* relationship is the same reason I didn't try to find you."

I kiss her forehead and pull her to me for a hug. "I don't like the thought of you walking this beach by yourself with a broken heart."

"It wasn't quite that dramatic," she murmurs, then laughs. "Actually, yeah. It was. I was twenty and I *was* heartbroken. But now I'm thirty, and I'm standing here on my favorite beach, with the man I've loved since I was a girl. I'm no poet, but I think that's pretty fucking romantic."

I laugh and lead her farther down the beach. "I agree. It's pretty fucking romantic. The tide is out. Let's go look around Haystack Rock to see what it brought in."

She nods and we spend the next hour carefully walking around rocks, pointing out ocean creatures. There are plenty more crabs and sea stars. Finally we walk back to the hotel and order room service so we can sit out on the deck to watch the sunset.

"Hello," the server says when the food is delivered. "I have dinner for two, and I brought up a complimentary pair of binoculars as well. The whales have been very active in the evenings."

"Awesome!" Mia exclaims and takes the binoculars. She hurries out onto the deck to look for whales while I wait for the server to set up dinner. When he leaves, I join her.

"See anything?"

"Not yet," she murmurs. "But you can bet your sweet ass I'll be sitting out here until dark, just in case."

"That's the plan." I smile when she turns around and sees the table set up on the deck. "You were too busy searching for Moby Dick to care that he was setting this up."

"It's fantastic." She raises her lips for a kiss, and I oblige. "I've been craving a crab Caesar salad."

"I'm sure it's incredibly fresh."

She takes a bite and nods happily. "Oh yeah. That's good stuff. Here, have a bite." She holds a bite up to my lips.

"Delicious."

"What's under there?" She points to a dish still covered.

"Dessert."

"What is it?"

"A surprise." I smirk when her eyes narrow. "You're not terribly patient, are you?"

"No." She laughs and continues eating her salad. "I can admit that I'm not patient. I hate surprises. I hate Christmas because my mom would wrap gifts weeks in advance. Our tree always went up Thanksgiving weekend, and the gifts would sit there for a month. It drove me nuts."

"This isn't a Christmas present," I remind her. "It's dessert."

"And I'm just about finished with my entrée," she says with an innocent smile.

"I'm not." She narrows her eyes again, making me laugh. I actually am just about finished, but I take my time with the last few bites, enjoying the way she squirms in her chair. "Now I'm looking forward to Christmas."

"Give me the sugar, and no one gets hurt."

"Threats." I cluck my tongue. "That's not very ladylike."

She raises a brow and waits as I keep my eyes on hers and raise the lid on the dessert.

"Cheesecake," she whispers.

"Strawberry."

She looks up at me. "You got two pieces."

"I can't expect you to share it. I mean, we just exerted ourselves on our beach walk. You need the calories."

"You know that I love you, right? Because I do."

"I know." I smile and hold a bite up to her lips. "I got the memo."

"Mm." She licks her lips and takes the fork from me. "Thank you."

Something behind her catches my eye. "Shit. Look."

Just as she turns around, a whale breaches the water and falls back in, making a spectacular splash. Then, five seconds later, another smaller one does the same.

"Oh, she has a baby," Mia cries, completely forgetting about the cake. I cover it back up as she reaches for the binoculars and races to the railing. "Oh my God, this is incredible. Look." She offers me the binoculars, but I shake my head.

I can see them. They're gorgeous.

"I count four whales right now," she says.

"The only time I've heard this much excitement in your voice is when you pick vegetables in your garden or pull a fresh pie from your oven," I say, and brush her hair to the side so I can kiss her neck. "You love this."

"Who wouldn't love this?" she asks. "Do you know how

many people go their whole lives without seeing a whale even once?"

"Do *you*?" I ask with a laugh.

"Okay, so I don't have exact statistics, but it's a lot. This is incredible, Camden."

She needs a place here.

I'll put that into motion next week. That'll be her Christmas gift this year. She deserves it.

"There are two babies," she says. "Oh my God, this is fantastic."

"You're fantastic," I whisper in her ear. Suddenly, she spins around and wraps her arms around me, holding on tightly. "What is it?"

"Thank you," she says and turns her big blue eyes up to me. "Thank you for this."

I tip my head down to kiss her lips. "This is entirely my pleasure, sweetheart. Watch your whales."

She kisses me again and turns back to watch the show in the water, and I know that I will never spend another day in my life without her.

She's mine.

Chapter Seventeen

~Mia~

I'm sure it's just a bug," I say to the doctor as she takes notes. "We arrived home from the beach last night, and I think it's probably just something I ate, or maybe even the flu."

"How long have you been feeling like this?" she asks, not looking up from her computer.

"Off and on for about a week, I guess. But it comes and goes."

"And when was your last period?"

I think back and can't remember, so I reach for my phone. "Let me check. It would have been about eight weeks since my last period." I frown. "But, I do remember that I had a spotty period last month."

"Not a full period?"

"No, but I'm under a ton of stress right now, and that usually makes my period weird." I shrug.

"Stress can definitely do that," she says with a smile. "It can even make you feel queasy."

"Yeah, I figured. But I thought I should come in, just in case."

She nods and finishes typing, then asks me to sit on the table with paper covering it. "Go ahead and lie down." She pushes her fingers into my stomach, then listens to my heart. "Sit up, please."

More poking and prodding and looking up my nose and into my ears.

"You seem pretty healthy," she says. "I know I say this every time I see you, but you could benefit from losing fifty pounds."

"Yes, but that's not why I'm here *today*."

"As your doctor, I need to remind you of that."

I roll my eyes behind her back and wait for her to tell me to go home and rest. But instead she hands me my slip and points down the hall.

"Take this and drop it off at the lab. Go ahead and leave a urine sample for me, and they'll draw some blood and send you back here."

This seems excessive for it being something I ate, but I shrug and follow directions. When the phlebotomist is finished poking forty-three holes in my arm, I make my way back to my room and sit for at least twenty minutes.

I shoot Riley a text.

Why is it that every time I go to the doctor, she writes OBE-SITY *as my diagnosis, even if I'm not here for that? Does my weight have anything at all to do with eating bad crab yesterday?*

I roll my eyes and read about rheumatoid arthritis on the poster opposite from where I'm sitting when Riley texts back.

What a bitch. I'm sorry you had bad crab! No one wants bad crabs. Ha ha!

I grin and put my phone away as the doctor walks back in with her laptop open and her glasses perched on the end of her nose.

"Well, we have figured this mystery out."

"Fantastic."

"You're pregnant."

I blink at her for a moment and then laugh. "Right. Oh gosh, that's funny. Anyway, what's up?"

"You're pregnant, Mia. We'll do an ultrasound to figure out exactly how far along you are, but I would guess between eight and ten weeks based on your last period."

"This can't be right." I shake my head and feel my cheeks flush. "I have a history of a false-positive pregnancy test. Maybe you should recheck."

"The blood test was positive," she replies. "I take it this isn't a planned pregnancy."

"No." I swallow hard. "No, it's not planned. We *always* use condoms."

"Are you sure?"

I scowl at her. "Of course I'm sure. I'm there, aren't I?"

"Well, even if you do use them every time without forgetting, they're only ninety-seven percent effective." She shrugs. "You seem to fall in that three percent."

"Lucky me." My voice is quiet and weak.

"I'm going to have my nurse wheel in the ultrasound machine, and we can take a quick look to see how far along you are. Unless you want to call the father so he can see it, too."

I stare at her as if she's just birthed a giraffe. "He doesn't even *know* yet. I don't think I'll call him and ask him to meet me here just so I can surprise him with a baby on the screen."

She nods and leaves for a moment. Within ten minutes, I'm in the stirrups with the lights out and have a wand stuck up my vagina. "That flutter is the heartbeat," she says, pointing to the screen.

"It's so little."

"Just about the size of a grain of sand," she says with a nod. "Everything looks good, and I'd estimate you're right at about ten weeks."

So, I pretty much got pregnant as soon as he and I hooked up.

I'm just a regular overachiever.

"But I've had periods," I say, confused. "I had a regular period *and* a spotty period."

"That can happen," she says with a nod. "It could be that you ovulated right after that first period, or you just had bleeding and didn't know. I've had patients who had periods their entire pregnancy. It's not unheard of."

"Huh."

After I'm cleaned up, have checked out, and am in my car, I sit and give myself permission to have a quick little freak-out session.

"What the fuck?" I stare at myself in the mirror. "I'm pregnant."

My heartbeat picks up, and my palms are suddenly

sweaty. I pull the photo from the ultrasound out of my purse and stare at it.

"You're quite the surprise," I whisper.

Should I panic? Should I be upset? I don't even know. At least now I *do* know that Camden loves me, and that we're doing so great together. But that's also the bad thing. We're *just* relearning each other and getting used to being together.

Now I'm going to throw a baby into the mix? What if he doesn't want kids? What if he doesn't want *me*?

I scowl at myself and shake my head. "Don't go there. He just spent a ton of time proving to you that he does want you. Wanting you isn't an issue."

Now I'm talking to myself in the third person.

Stop that. Just go home and tell him. He's coming up with some new recipes for the show, so you know he's home. Stop at the store and get him a card or, I don't know, a freaking bouquet of flowers or something, and tell him that he's going to be a daddy.

And pray that he doesn't run away screaming.

That thought actually makes me laugh. He's not going to do that. He's a good man, and even if we don't end up together forever, he'll be a great dad.

I nod and turn the car on, impressed that I'm so calm about this.

Then again, I've been here before. He didn't freak out last time. He *married* me for crying out loud.

I call Camden, using the hands-free option on my car.

"Hi, beautiful," he says in greeting, making me smile.

"Hi there. How's it going?"

"Pretty well. I think I have the Italian episode figured out."

"Oh, that sounds so good. Can we practice that one to-night?"

"If you like," he replies. I can hear the smile in his voice. "What's up?"

"Well, I'm on my way home, and I wanted to make sure you're going to be there when I get there."

"I should be. I don't have plans to leave."

"Great."

"Why?"

"I have something to tell you, but I want to do it in person."

"You can just tell me."

I laugh. "No, I can't. I *want* to tell you in person. Who's impatient now?"

He laughs. "Okay. I can wait."

"I have one errand to run, and then I'll be home. And don't worry. Just remember I love you, and everything's fine. I'll see you soon."

"I love you too, babe."

He hangs up and I turn into the Target parking lot. I want to get him a present, but I have no idea what. So, I spend ten minutes on Pinterest, trying to find the best way to tell him. I can't decide, so I just go inside and walk through the baby section, getting kind of mushy and excited. I wish I could tell one of the girls and ask them for help, but I'd better tell him first.

It's important that I do this the *right* way.

I find a onesie that says *So the Adventure Begins*, and I think that's pretty perfect.

This is definitely going to be an adventure.

So I snatch that up, along with a card that's blank inside. When I get to the car, I write, *Congratulations, Daddy* inside the card and put it in a fun gift bag with the onesie.

That's pretty good for spur of the moment, if I do think so myself.

I feel like the past few days have taken our relationship to a brand-new place. The past is *finally* in the past, and we love each other. I have no qualms at all about telling him about this baby.

I wonder what would have happened ten years ago if I *had* been pregnant? Would we still be married, or would we have divorced, making us split time with the kiddo? Would we hate each other by now?

Because let's be honest, we were *so* young then, and obviously not great with communication. I don't see how that could have lasted long term.

"It doesn't matter," I mutter and flip the radio on. The freeway is busy, but moving well, and I'm excited to get home to Camden. I'm not even nervous.

"Holy fuck, I'm going to have a *baby*."

I do a little happy dance in my seat just as the guy ahead of me switches lanes.

But the person ahead of *him* is stopped dead, and I don't have time to stop.

Loud noise. Airbag in my face.

Nothing.

IT FEELS LIKE I'm swimming in really thick water. I can't move. Sounds are really slow and far away.

I open my eyes, and it's like being hit by a hammer. Loud noises, people bustling around. It smells horrible.

"Miss?"

"Huh?"

"Don't move." I glance to my left and see a guy in his twenties looking in at me. He's wearing a hat and suspenders. "We're cutting you out of there."

"What's happening?"

"You rear-ended the car in front of you going pretty fast."

I frown and cry out at the pain in my head.

"Your car is crushed in. You also got hit from the rear. So we have to cut you out of here."

"Shit." The light hurts. Everything hurts. "Baby."

"Did you have a baby in the car?"

"No." I lick my lips, unable to open my eyes, the light hurts so badly. "Pregnant."

"She's pregnant!" he yells to someone. I'm in the water again, fighting to stay awake, but the water is warm and it doesn't hurt here. I let myself slip back under, until there's nothing.

"WAKE UP, MIA."

"No." It's loud. I don't want to get up and go to work. I'd rather lie here next to Camden. Maybe we can just have sex all day. That would be fun, but I have a killer headache. "Head hurts."

"I know, sweetheart, but I need you to wake up. You have a concussion."

I open an eye, and I'm thrust into a nightmare. Two men

are looking down at me, and it feels like I'm speeding in a car.

"What's happening?"

"Do you remember me?" one of the men asks. "You talked to me when you woke up in the car, do you remember?"

"Sort of." I wince. "My head is killing me."

"You hit it pretty good," he says with a smile. "But it looks like that's the worst of it. Mia, I need you to tell me what day it is."

"September something." I frown. "My mouth is dry."

"September what?"

"Tenth? It's Wednesday."

"Good girl," he says and holds a straw to my mouth. "You can have a sip of this. What year is it?"

"2018."

He nods and looks up at the other guy. "How's her BP?"

"High, but not scary."

"My parents."

"I called your mom," he says. "I found your phone, and *Mom* was listed as your emergency contact."

"Good."

I try to swallow, but everything in me hurts.

"Someone in front of me changed lanes, and the car in front of them was stopped dead. I had no warning."

"That's what the guy said who rear-ended you. He's fine, he was able to slam on his breaks."

I try to move my head, but it's strapped to a board. "I can't move."

"We need you to have some scans done to make sure you

don't have a spinal injury," he says. "But the fact that you're staying awake and talking to me is a very good sign. You scared me when you passed out on me again."

"I think I scared me, too," I whisper. "I'm really tired."

"Stay awake, Mia," the other guy says.

"You two are ridiculously good looking."

They both smile down at me. "Is that a requirement to be a fire fighter or EMT? That you have to be hot so you can make calendars and bring in a bunch of money in calendar sales?"

"She found us out." He presses some gauze to my head and comes away with blood. "You have quite the head wound here. I hope blood doesn't make you queasy."

"No choice, I guess," I reply, and immediately feel queasy. "I'm always nauseated these days."

"How far along are you?" he asks, surprising me. I blink at him for a moment, and he says, "You said you're pregnant."

"Oh God, I'm pregnant. Around ten weeks."

He nods and exchanges a look with the other guy that isn't encouraging.

"Am I going to lose it?"

"I don't know, Mia. I'm not a doctor, but I do know that they'll do everything they can to make sure that you don't."

I nod, tears falling down my cheeks now. "Can I call someone?"

"Who?"

"Camden." I swallow. "I don't know if they'll think to call him right away."

"I'll call him." I nod as he finds Camden's name in my phone and holds it to my ear.

"I was wondering where you are."

"I don't want you to freak out."

"What's happening?"

"I'm okay."

"Mia, tell me what's happening."

"I'm in an ambulance. I was in an accident, and we're going to the hospital." I can't stop the tears from flowing now. "Will you please meet me there?"

"Oh my God, of course. Which hospital?"

"I don't know. Which hospital?"

The EMT takes my phone and talks to Camden, giving him the name of the hospital, and how far out we are from there, which isn't far, and then he presses the phone back to my ear.

"You listen to me, Mia. You're going to be okay. I'm on my way to meet you. I love you, baby."

"I l-l-love you too," I whisper. "I have so much to tell you."

"You're going to tell me very soon. You're so brave, my love. Just hang in there, okay?"

"Okay."

He's gone, and I'm left staring at Mr. EMT. "Are we almost there?"

"Yes, ma'am. Just a few more minutes."

"I'm really sleepy."

"Mia, we don't want you to sleep. You have a head injury."

"I can't help it."

Chapter Eighteen

~Camden~

I hang up the phone and reach for my keys, trying to keep the ball of panic down when Trevor calls.

"Mia's been in an accident," I say in greeting.

"I know. I was calling to tell you. We're all on our way to the hospital. Do you want me to swing by and pick you up?"

"No, I'll get there faster on my own." I run down the stairs of the house to my car. "Have you heard what her condition is?"

"Just that she's stable and being rushed to Emanuel Hospital," he replies. "We will meet you there."

He hangs up and I immediately dial Steph's number.

"Do you miss me already?" she asks when she answers.

"Where are you?"

"Camden? I thought you were . . . never mind. What's happening?" Her voice is sober now.

"I'm on my way to the hospital. Mia's been in a car accident."

"Oh, God. I'm in Olympia. I can be down there in like an hour and a half."

I take a deep breath. "Okay. I don't know much now. I spoke with her for a minute when they had her in the ambulance and she sounded scared, out of it. It's my worst nightmare."

"I know. I know. I'm on my way. Keep me posted if you find out more."

I give her the hospital information and then hang up, just as I'm arriving at the hospital. I find the ER, park, and run inside to find that most everyone has beat me here.

Mia's parents are sitting with Landon and Cami. Riley and Trevor have just walked in ahead of me. Addie, Jake, Kat and a man that I assume is her husband, are sitting nearby.

"Camden." Addie walks to me and offers me a hug. "She's here, but no one is allowed to go back with her yet."

"They're running scans and such," Landon says, his face grim. "She's pretty beat up, but we don't know how badly she's beat up quite yet. The lab and the imaging departments are backed up, so they warned us that it could be a couple of hours before we know something."

"And they won't let anyone back to at least sit with her?" I ask, the anger setting up root in my belly. "When I spoke to her, she was terrified."

"She's unconscious," Cami replies. Her eyes are red and swollen from crying. "We were told that either when she wakes up, or they have more information, we can go back with her."

"I fucking hate waiting," Riley mutters and rubs her hands over her face.

Less than an hour later, Steph comes rushing through the doors, her eyes wide and frantic until she finds me. She hugs me and asks how she is.

"We don't know," I reply, rubbing circles on her back. "We haven't been given an update, but she's unconscious."

"She's going to be okay," Steph says and looks around the room at all of Mia's family and friends. "I'm his sister."

"We assumed so," Addie says with a smile. She briefly introduces everyone, and then turns back to us. "Did you drive all the way from Seattle?"

"I was working in Olympia today, so I only had half as far to drive."

"You still made good time," Jake replies. "We probably don't want to know how fast you were driving."

"No," Steph replies. "You don't. Also, aren't you Jake Knox?"

"This is my husband," Addie says with a smile.

"It's Jake Knox," I reply. "She had a massive crush on you back in the day."

"Hell, on *this* day," Steph says and shrugs. "I'm happily married too, by the way, but yeah. Big fan."

Jake grins, and just then the doctor comes through the double doors. She looks tired as she scans the waiting area.

"Mr. and Mrs. Palazzo?"

"That's us." Mia's parents stand. Landon joins them, and the doctor approaches them.

"Do you want to go somewhere private to talk?" she asks.

"No," Landon says. "Everyone here is family."

The doctor nods. "I'm Dr. Miller, and I'm Mia's physician today. Your daughter is very lucky. She was in a car accident, as you know. She rear-ended the car ahead of her at a high speed. The police estimate that she was going at around forty-five miles per hour."

"Jesus," Trevor mutters.

"Then, a man rear-ended *her*. He wasn't going as fast, which is probably what saved her life. The car crumpled like an accordion, so the first responders had to cut her out of the car.

"We've done a CT scan and taken several X-rays. It appears that she has one broken rib, some bruising on her chest from the seat belt, and lacerations on her head where she hit the airbag. She has a concussion, which was concerning because we couldn't get her to stay awake, but she seems to be doing better now."

"Is she going to be okay?" Cami asks, holding on to Landon's hand for dear life.

Steph is standing beside me, also holding on to my hand.

"Yes," Dr. Miller says with a nod. "She's going to be just fine. I think we'll keep her here overnight, just so we can watch that concussion, but she's going to make a full recovery.

"It's going to take about thirty more minutes to get her settled in her room, and then you are all welcome to go in and see her. I would recommend no more than four of you at a time, as the room isn't that big."

She turns to leave, but then stops short and turns back.

"I almost forgot. The baby is fine, too. She's going to need to monitor things for a few weeks, but I don't think there will be any trouble."

She walks away, and I'm stunned.

"What baby?" Steph asks me.

"I have no idea," I murmur. My God, is *that* what she was hurrying home to tell me? I look around and all eyes are on me, but there's nothing that I can say, given that I simply don't know.

Did she just find out today? Has she known for a while?

"What are you thinking?" Steph asks quietly.

"I don't know what to think."

I just shake my head at the others and sigh, then rub my hands over my face in frustration.

"I take it he didn't know either," Kat murmurs. I can hear other voices around me, but I've tuned them all out. All I know for sure is, the woman I love more than anything is lying in a hospital bed alone, that she's apparently carrying a baby that I didn't know about, and *I can't get to her.*

"We're going to go," Addie says and everyone but Mia's parents, brother, and Cami nod. "Now that we know she's okay, we'll go and come back later this evening or tomorrow morning. Just please keep us posted if anything changes."

"We will," Landon says. "Thanks for being here."

I'm hugged and assured that everything is okay as they leave, but I barely feel it. I need to see Mia. I need to ask her a million questions.

Not even ten minutes later, a nurse comes out to escort us back to Mia's room. Stephanie and I lag behind, entering the room last. Mia's parents immediately rush to her and hug her, her mother crying.

"Oh, bambina," she says. "You scared me. How are you? Do you need anything?"

Mia searches the room for me, and when her eyes meet mine, they soften, but she doesn't ask for me. Instead, she just starts to talk about the accident.

"It was stupid. The guy changed lanes to move to a faster moving one, but I couldn't see that traffic was stopped ahead of him. And that's really all I remember."

Her head is wrapped in gauze. Her arm is in a sling, and her white skin matches the sheets on the bed.

She's hooked up to dozens of wires and monitors. Her heartbeat is thumping in the room.

"It was scary," she whispers, and her mother hugs her again.

"I want to hear about this baby," her father says. Mia's eyes immediately fly to mine again, and she shakes her head.

"Not now."

"Were you *ever* going to tell anyone?" Steph asks, her hands on her hips and her face a mask of pure anger. "Do you know how horrible it is that Camden found out this way?"

"Stop," I say, holding on to her elbow to keep her from advancing on Mia. "This is *not* the time for this."

"I know you're hurt," Steph continues. "And I'm so relieved that you're going to be okay. But Mia, *again*? After everything you've been through with my brother, you're going to do this to him again?"

"Do what?" Cami asks with a frown. "You don't know that she's done *anything* to your brother."

"She knows." Steph nods and then shakes her head in disgust. "I can't believe that we'd all started to trust you. To think that you've grown up, and it would be different this time."

Mia glares at Steph for a moment, then turns her gaze to me.

"You don't get to talk to her like that," I tell my sister. "Look at me."

"No, I want to hear from *her*."

"You don't get to hear from me," Mia says. "First of all, it's none of your fucking business; and two, don't you think I'd rather tell the father of my child that he's going to be a daddy before I tell anyone else? You're making assumptions, and maybe it's out of fear. I know that car accidents are probably a trigger for you, given how you lost your parents. But you don't get to shame me in front of my family and my boyfriend, Steph. If you'd all get the hell out of here, and give Camden and me a moment to ourselves, I can properly tell him that he's going to be a daddy."

She's so fucking magnificent when she's fighting. When she's fighting for me, and for what's right for *us*.

Landon kisses her forehead, takes Cami's hand and leads her out of the room. Their parents do the same, and finally, I look down at Steph and gesture for her to get the fuck out of here.

When they're gone, I latch the door closed, but before I can walk to Mia, the doctor bustles in.

"Oh, I'm happy to see that the family has left you be for a while," she says with a smile. "You've had a rough afternoon, and I'd like to keep you as calm as possible. Are you the daddy?" she asks, looking at me.

"He is," Mia replies, but won't look me in the eyes.

"Well, this monitor here is Mia's heartbeat. And this one is the baby. As you can see, the baby's is much faster than mama's."

I'm still struck dumb. I'm watching everything unfold as if it's a movie, and I'm the outsider.

Finally, the doctor leaves; and I once again latch the door closed behind her, and turn around to take Mia in.

She's even paler, if that's possible. Her dark hair is haloed around her head. Her fingers are fiddling with the blanket in her lap. Finally, her blue eyes meet mine and she smiles softly.

"So, I have something to tell you."

Chapter Nineteen

~Mia~

"I'm all ears," Camden says, and leans back against the closed door, his arms crossed over his chest. He's not frowning. He doesn't look mad. But he doesn't look happy either, and that's what scares the fuck out of me.

"Well, you know that I wasn't feeling like myself for a while, and I went to the doctor today."

He nods.

"I figured I just had a bug or maybe I'd eaten something that didn't agree with me. My doctor drew some blood and took a urine sample, and then surprised the shit out of me when she said I'm going to—" I swallow hard—"have a baby."

He bites his lip and I keep talking because I can't read his expression, and I feel like I need to fill the heavy silence in the room, even though I haven't done anything wrong.

"This isn't how I wanted you to find out," I continue. "At first I was nervous, but then I was looking forward to seeing you. I really need you to tell me how you're feeling about this."

"How do *you* feel about it?" he asks, finally speaking. He uncrosses his arms and tucks his hands in his pockets, but he doesn't come to me, and for the first time in my life, I want someone to touch me *so fucking badly* that it hurts.

"I don't know," I admit, and hate that I feel on the verge of tears. "They gave me some pretty good pain meds that they said wouldn't hurt the baby, so I'm a little jumbled. I feel like I haven't had the chance to fully process it all. I just wanted to make sure that I did it right this time."

"Did what right?"

"*Everything.* That I told you before I told anyone else. It helped that I actually had it confirmed by a doctor this time, and not just a stick to pee on."

He nods, and if I'm not mistaken, the corner of his mouth tips up in what could be the beginning of a smile, and it gives me hope that he's not completely pissed off at me.

"So, I was excited to get home to see you and give you the news. I don't see this as a bad thing. But then the next thing I knew, I was in an ambulance with a killer headache. And now I'm here, in this *really* uncomfortable bed. Your sister accused me of lying to you again, and you're standing way over there. You might as well be in Florida right now, you're so distant and that just scares me."

"I'm right here," he says and finally walks to me. He sits

at the side of my bed and takes my hand in his, brushing his thumb over my knuckles. He looks over at the baby's heart-beat. "That's the baby?"

"That's what they tell me."

He nods and watches it for a moment, then lets out a long sigh.

"Can you scoot over just a smidge?"

I oblige him, and he threads his way around the cords attached to me, and pulls me into his arms. I can't hold the tears back, and I don't want to. I cry against his chest while he drags his fingers up and down my arm.

"You're okay, baby," he says and plants his lips on my head. "How do you feel?"

"My head hurts," I reply with a sniff. "I'm sore every-where. I'm afraid that you think I was trying to keep this from you and you're angry with me."

"I'm not angry," he says and tips my chin up to look at him. "I'm not angry at you."

"You haven't been exactly warm and fuzzy."

"I know, I'm sorry. Everything's jumbled in my head. Of course I was worried and scared. So fucking scared, Mia. I just finally have you back in my life. I can't lose you again. If anything were to happen to you, I just don't know what I would do.

"And I admit that today was way too similar to the day we lost Mom and Dad. I'd just got off the phone with you, and then suddenly you're calling me again and you're on the way to the hospital. I didn't know how badly you were hurt, and once I got here, we couldn't get back to you. Steph came down from Olympia where she was working today to be with me."

"Was anyone unkind to you?" I ask, ready to kick some ass.

"No. Your friends and your parents were fine. They were scared, too. And then the doctor came out to let your family know that you'd be fine, and that the *baby* would be fine."

"Fuck," I whisper and brush a tear off my cheek. Crying only made my head hurt worse, but it was a cleansing cry. "I'm sorry you found out like that."

"Everyone turned to stare at me, but I didn't know either, so I didn't know what to say."

"There was nothing to say," I insist. "Jesus, Camden, I'd just found out not even thirty minutes before I called you to let you know that I was on my way home. It's not like I've carried this secret around with me for weeks, waiting for the perfect moment to tell you or something."

"I'm glad," he admits and kisses my head again. "And I'm so fucking relieved that you're okay. That you're both okay."

I relax against him, enjoying the way his arms feel around me, relieved to be here with him. I can't help but let out a soft chuckle.

"What's so funny?"

"I can only imagine the looks my parents and Landon must have sent you when the doctor said the baby would be okay."

I look up to find him smiling down at me.

"It was awkward, that's for sure."

"I'm sorry," I reply and kiss his chest. "I'll fill them in on the specifics. It's crazy because three of us are pregnant at the same time."

"Who else?" he asks.

"Cami and Riley are both expecting." I smile up at him. "It's fun that we'll be doing this at the same time."

"Are you happy about it?" he asks.

"Yeah. I know it's not ideal, but we love each other." I shrug and feel my eyelids getting heavy. "We will figure it all out."

"We'll get married right away, of course," he says, and I sit up, immediately wide awake again.

"No."

"Bullshit. You and this baby will have my name. I was going to propose anyway, Mia."

Something softens inside me. "You were?"

"I swear, I was."

"That's sweet. But I'm still not marrying you until after this baby is born." He narrows his eyes menacingly, and I keep talking. "Glare at me all day long, Camden, but I will not bend on this. I'm not going to have people saying that I'm trapping you into marriage."

"Your past actions aren't exactly indicative of someone trying to trap me."

"I don't care. When we get married, it'll be because we want to, not because of a baby."

"For the record, I don't like it and I don't agree."

I life my chin stubbornly and he kisses it.

"Fine. We'll wait until after the baby's born."

"WHAT'S THAT?" CAMDEN asks three months later. We're in my doctor's office for an ultrasound, and he's been harassing the ultrasound tech for the past ten minutes.

"That's the placenta," she says. She's measuring and marking things, and once in a while when she sweeps past the baby I can see the fluttering of the heart. "It's the appropriate size for how far along you are."

I grin at Camden, but he's enthralled with the ultrasound screen.

"What's this?"

"That's your baby's foot," she replies. "Five little toes."

"Aww, it has toes," I say to Camden.

"Of course it does." He points to the screen. "What's that?"

"Stop asking the poor woman what everything is," I say, squeezing his hand.

"It's okay," she says with a grin. "He's excited, and that's a good thing. That's the baby's knee. And in a minute here, I can tell you the sex if you want."

"No."

"Yes."

Camden scowls at me. "Of course we want to know."

"Not *today*. We have to keep it a secret until the gender reveal party on Saturday."

"This is ridiculous," Camden says, shaking his head. "Just tell us."

"No," I repeat. "Cami's excited because we get to find out the sex of our baby *and* Riley's baby on the same day. Just let her have this, babe."

"Fine." He glances at the tech. "Just whisper it to me."

"No," I say, laughing my ass off. "And stop making me laugh. I have to pee like crazy and I'd rather not do it here."

Twenty minutes later, we're in the car with a sealed envelope with the gender of the baby inside.

"You didn't ask her when I was peeing, did you?"

"I wouldn't do that," he replies as he starts the car and drives toward home. "How do you feel?"

"Like you already know the sex of the baby and I don't."

"You don't know that that's true."

"Damn it, Camden."

He grins over at me and kisses my knuckles. "I love you, Mia. You're the most beautiful woman in the world."

"I love you too." I stare at the envelope in my lap. "I hate surprises."

He tips his head back and laughs. "You asked for this one, sweetheart."

"Saturday better hurry up and get here."

"It'll be here quickly. What do you want for dinner?"

"McDonald's."

He scrunches up his face. "Ugh. Why?"

"I don't know, I've been craving McDonald's fries for a week now."

"Your boyfriend is a celebrity gourmet chef who could make you *anything*, and you want McDonald's fries?"

"And some sweet tea," I confirm with a nod. "And maybe some chicken nuggets."

"I draw a line on the nuggets. I can't have our child consuming that stuff." He shakes his head and looks over at me in horror. "Are you shitting me right now?"

"Totally. I want chicken alfredo for dinner."

"Thank God."

THIS IS A *lot* of pregnant women in the same room," I say to Addie on Saturday afternoon. We decided that the only place that was big enough for everyone was at Addie and Jake's house, since we couldn't shut the restaurant down on a Saturday afternoon. The whole house is decorated in pink and blue with touches of grey. "The decorations are really pretty."

"Thanks," Addie says with a grin. "I hired it out, of course, but they did a great job. In addition to cake, we have sugar cookies decorated to look like baby stuff. They're little works of art."

"I think Camden's already eaten three." I smile at the man in question who's standing across the room talking with Landon, my dad, and Mac.

"Are you nervous to find out the sex?" Riley asks as she joins us, sipping on sparkling water in a champagne flute.

"No, I'm excited. How about you?"

"I'm excited too. Trevor thought this was dumb, so I had to hide the envelope from him." She smiles and rubs her hand over her barely protruding belly. "It's cute that he's excited."

"Both Trevor and Camden look antsy," Jake says as he joins

us. "And I don't blame them. This is dumb. Why couldn't they find out at their appointments?"

"Because this is fun," Addie says, rolling her eyes. "If I'd been thinking, we would have done the same thing when I was pregnant with Ella."

"You can do it with the next one," Jake says and kisses his wife, then exchanges an intimate, happy smile with her.

"Addie."

She looks over at me and shrugs. "Yeah, I'm knocked up again. But today isn't about me."

"Oh my God, this is so amazing. And it's about *all* of us today, so yes, you will announce it."

"Announce what?" Cami asks from across the room.

I level my gaze on Addie and Jake, and finally Addie shrugs and announces to the now quiet room, "We're going to have another baby."

The whooping, and hollering, and congratulations are loud and enthusiastic.

"We're all just a fertile group of people," Landon says with a happy shrug. "Atta girl, blondie."

Finally, after more hugs and laughter, Cami calls everyone to attention.

"Thanks for letting us do this," she says. "I know it's hard to wait to find out the sex of your baby. I couldn't do it."

"Yeah, you didn't let us do this for you when you and Landon found out you're having a girl."

Cami just shrugs. "Like I said, it's hard. So thanks for letting Addie and me throw this party, and thank you to everyone for coming.

"Since Riley is due first, we're going to let her and Trevor cut their cake first. If the filling is pink, it's a girl. And, of course, if it's blue, it's a boy."

"We've had all girls in this family so far," Kat says. "Do us a solid and let me buy some cute boy things."

Riley and Trevor both hold the cake cutter, as if they're cutting a wedding cake. Suddenly, Riley tears up and just leans against Trevor, who kisses her head.

"What is it?"

"Pink," he says and holds up his slice of cake. "We're having a girl."

Camden joins me at our cake, as we all applaud and yell out congratulations to Riley and Trevor.

"Tell me," I whisper to Camden, who just grins. "You know, don't you?"

"We're both about to know in ten seconds."

"Just tell me. You know I hate secrets."

"Stop whispering and cut the damn cake," Landon calls out.

We hold the knife and cut into the cake and plate our slice, and I frown, confused.

"I don't get it." I look up at Camden, who just has tears in his eyes. "What's happening?"

"What's wrong?"

"We have both," I reply and hold up the cake. Every face in the room drops in surprise.

Camden's sister exclaims, "Does that mean it's twins?"

"Holy shit." I stare up at Camden in horror, but he's still just grinning with that goofy look, and the next thing I know, I'm swept up in his arms and he's whispering in my ear.

"One was hiding behind the other before," he says and kisses my cheek. "We're having a boy *and* a girl."

"No way."

"Way, sweetheart. We got a twofer."

I've never been hugged so much in my life. Over the next thirty minutes, we're shuffled from person to person, and finally when we've talked to everyone, Camden holds his hand up to get our attention.

"Let me tell you what happened," he begins. "We went for the ultrasound the other day, and I didn't want to wait to know the sex. So while Mia was in the bathroom, I persuaded the tech to tell me, promising to keep it a secret.

"But what she told me instead was that it was *twins*. She refused to tell me what the sexes were of the babies. She said I had to find out with Mia. But she wanted me to be able to explain to you all today that when we had previously gone in for ultrasounds to make sure that everything was still okay after the accident, one of the babies must have been hiding behind the other. I guess it happens sometimes." He looks down at me and rests his hand on my belly. "I'm sorry I didn't tell you, I just knew it was going to be one hell of a surprise."

"You're not kidding." I rest my hand over his and try to process it all. "Two babies?"

"Two babies."

Chapter Twenty

~Camden~

These babies are trying to kill me," Mia says from the passenger seat of my car. We've had a mild winter, and she's starting to go stir-crazy now that she's in the final month of her pregnancy. Since there hasn't been any snow, I decided it was safe to take a quick trip over to the beach for the weekend. I have a surprise for her.

"I don't think the babies are homicidal," I remind her, and lay my hand on her round belly. She's seemed to get bigger overnight these past few days, not that I'd dare say that to her. She's also glowing and the most beautiful woman I've ever seen. "How do you feel? Maybe we shouldn't have come."

"I needed to get out of that house," she says with a sigh. "*Someone* won't let me work anymore."

"You're carrying twins, my love. You can't be on your

feet for ten hours like you used to. You're lucky that the doctor hasn't put you on bed rest."

"I'm healthy. The babies are healthy, and my blood pressure is normal. I'm fine. How is it going at Seduction?" she asks and tucks her hair behind her ear. "Is what's-her-face still always late?"

"No," I reply. "Are you sure you're okay with me taking over your kitchen?"

"Better you than some yayhoo I don't know."

"You love the chef you hired," I remind her with a smile. "He would have been capable."

"Are you saying you don't want to do it?" Her eyes are wide when they find mine, and I feel like an ass.

"No. I enjoy being there. And if it means that you're able to relax at home, I'll be there every minute of every day."

"Well let's not get crazy," she says, her voice dry. "I mean, I still want to see you on a regular basis. But it makes me feel better knowing that you're there. You know how I'd want things to be done, and you'll make sure it happens."

"You came in three times last week. It's not like you'll never be there again."

"I'm dramatic," she says with a shrug. "This whole pregnancy thing has my hormones out of control. And there are *two* of them, which means I'm outnumbered."

"I love that you consider our children your enemy."

"Only where my body is concerned," she says with a sigh. "I've lost more weight than I've gained. I mean, I know that I needed to lose some weight, but I don't think you're supposed to do that when you're pregnant."

"Who told you that you needed to lose weight?"

She laughs and takes my hand, kissing it. "Oh, you're so sweet. Only just about everyone, Camden. All my life. And now that I'm allowed to gain a pound or two, I'm losing it because I can't keep food down to save my life."

"How is the nausea today?"

"Not horrible," she says. "It calmed down a bit this trimester. It's mostly bad smells that set me off now."

"Like when I burned the steaks the other night." I wince. "Sorry about that."

"Well, you were putting a crib together and I fell asleep. I would say that was a joint venture."

She laughs and looks out the passenger window. "It was a good call to go to the beach this weekend. I can't believe there's no snow between Portland and Cannon Beach."

"It's been a warm winter," I agree. "I'm glad your doctor gave us the go-ahead to travel."

She's silent for a long moment, and I glance over to find her biting her bottom lip.

"Mia."

"What?"

"You did ask the doctor, right?"

"Well, I called, and I asked the doctor a question," she says. "So, when I told you that, it wasn't a lie."

"But you didn't ask her if it was safe for you to go out of town for the weekend."

"I wanted to come," she says. "The doctor said before that I'm not allowed to *fly*. This isn't flying. It's only an hour, hour and a half tops. I drive that far to the mall."

"No, you don't."

"You know what I mean."

"Jesus, Mia, what if something happens?"

"Nothing's going to happen. This has been a perfectly normal pregnancy for twins. I'm just nauseated sometimes, and I've been having Braxton Hicks, but that's not a big deal."

"What's a Braxton Hicks?"

"False labor," she says with a shrug.

"What? You've been in *labor*?"

"*False* labor," she says. "It's just contractions that help get your body ready for delivery. It's not *real* labor. I mean, it hurts like a mother fucker all the same, but I'm not having these babies for a long time yet."

"Three weeks," I remind her. "You're due in only three weeks."

"Thank God," she whispers. "I'm ready to meet them. They've been kicking, and jumping, and playing soccer with my bladder. It's time they came out to say hello."

"Well, it would be ideal if they stay where they are until we get home," I reply and take the exit off Highway 101 that takes us to the surprise I want to show her.

"I thought we were staying at that same hotel we found last time."

"We do have a reservation there, but I found another place that might be nice. We can just take a look at it first, and if we don't like it, go on to the hotel."

"Okay."

I pull into a driveway that leads to a house that was built

in the 1920s, but has recently been renovated from top to bottom with all of the most up-to-date conveniences.

"A house?"

"Yes." I get out and walk around to her side, helping her up out of the car. She frowns and rubs her hand over her belly. "What's wrong?"

"Nothing," she says and takes a long, deep breath. "The Braxton Hicks usually happen when I stand up. I'm okay."

She smiles up at me, and I lead her to the front door where the realtor is waiting.

"Oh, would we be renting this from you?" Mia asks, offering her hand to shake.

"I'm going to let Camden explain everything to you," Fiona, the realtor, replies. "Go ahead and look around. I'll be waiting out here."

"Thank you," I reply and lead Mia inside. "I've only seen the place online. Let's wander through and see what you think."

"Well, it's beautiful," she says. "I love these high ceilings, and the crown molding looks like it's original."

"I believe it is." She nods and wanders through to the kitchen where she stops and stares through the windows.

"Oh, Camden."

"What's wrong?"

"Nothing, look at this view!"

I walk up behind her and wrap my arms around her, resting my hands on her belly.

"Do you like it?" I whisper.

"We're literally above the water. Of course I like it. The trek down to the sand might be harder for me this time, but I'm happy to stay up here and watch the storms come in and out." She turns and smiles up at me. "Thank you."

"Well, there's more to say. And more to see."

I lead her through the living area and up the stairs to show her three bedrooms—each with its own bathroom—another living space, and the master bedroom with a balcony that faces the water.

"Never mind, I'll just sit up here all weekend," she says with a smile.

"Do you like it?"

"What's not to like?"

"If you love it, it's yours."

Her eyes go wide and she stares up at me for a moment before frowning. "What?"

"It's yours. The paperwork is ready for me to sign. I've been looking for the perfect place since the last time we were here. You are the most alive when you're on this beach, and I wanted to give it to you."

"Wow, this is the best push present ever."

"Excuse me?"

"Oh," she waves me off. "A push present is a thing that men get the mother for having the baby. This one is impressive."

"I didn't even know that was a thing."

She smiles. "Are you serious? Because punking me like this when I'm forty-seven months pregnant with twins is *not* okay."

"I'm totally serious. I'm prepared to pay cash for it today, as long as it's what you want. I've had inspections done, along with appraisals. It's a go if you are."

"I'm in," she says and tips her head up for a kiss. "Thank you *so much*. This is incredible."

"*You're* incredible," I reply and walk with her back to the kitchen. "I figured you'd want to replace the stovetop and fridge with something more commercial grade."

"Eventually," she says, nodding. "But this will all work great for now."

She suddenly holds on to the countertop, doubling over. "Holy shit."

"What is it?"

"These stupid *fake* contractions are ridiculous."

"Mia, that doesn't sound right."

"I'm fine," she says, holding her hand up and breathing through the pain. But then suddenly there's a splash. "Fuck. My water broke."

"Come on," I reply grimly. "We're going to the hospital.

"Fake labor my ass."

FOUR HOURS. THAT'S how long it took from the time we got Mia to the hospital in nearby Seaside, Oregon, until the moment our daughter was born, and then our son just six minutes later.

I wasn't sure if I'd survive it. I've never seen a human being go through that much pain before and live to tell about it.

I thought I respected her before, but now I'm just in awe of her.

"How is he?" Mia asks. She's holding our daughter, Elizabeth, and I'm holding Ethan. We weren't expecting them to come so soon, so we didn't have Mia's hospital suitcase in the car with us, but the hospital has happily loaned us all of the blankets and supplies we need until ours arrive.

"He's gorgeous," I reply with a grin, and sit on the bed at her hip so we can both see them. "They're so tiny."

"Not too tiny though," she says. "At almost seven pounds each, that's a lot of baby to come out of my body today."

"I'm so fucking proud of you," I whisper and smile down at her. "Seriously, you were a goddamn rockstar today."

"I was so pissed when we got here and they said I was too far into it to get the epidural," she replies. "And I'm mad at myself for being impatient and pouting. Maybe we shouldn't have come. I wish my doctor could have delivered them."

"Hey, the most important thing right now is that all three of you are safe and healthy, whether you delivered in Portland or Chicago."

"I wasn't allowed to fly. Chicago was out."

"You're a smart ass."

"Oh yeah. A complete smart ass."

"You're marrying me now," I say, and earn a scowl from her. "That was the deal. We had to wait until the babies were born."

"You didn't even ask," she says. "Don't think that you can just start demanding things."

"You said you didn't *want* the proposal, and that you would marry me after they came."

"No, I—"

"Where are my grandchildren?" Mia's mother asks as she and her husband walk into the room. Before we know it, both babies are scooped up by them, and they're cooing over them.

"Oh, what a sweetheart," Mia's dad says. He glances up at me. "She has your nose."

"Poor kid," I reply with a grin. "Is everyone else here?"

"Most are," he replies. "You should go out and say hello. They're only allowing three people back here at a time."

"Do you mind if I go out so Landon can come in?" I ask Mia, who smiles happily.

"Sure. It was kind of nice having a few moments alone with our little family. But I'm excited for everyone to meet them."

"I love you," I reply and kiss her gently. "And I'll be back soon."

"I love you, too."

"You're totally marrying me."

"Go get my brother."

ELIZABETH IS SLEEPING, but Ethan decided he wanted some company at three o'clock in the morning, so here I sit, rocking him in the dark in the nursery.

"Were you lonely?" I whisper. He's sleepy, but I know if I put him down he'll cry again, and I'd rather he didn't wake Lizzy. Mia needs her sleep. "You've always been the one who wants to be held." Ethan grins up at me. "I know. You're a social guy. But at two months old, it would be awesome if you'd sleep through the night."

He just grins and bites on his fist. I honestly don't mind getting up with them. I know these days won't last long.

"I'm letting your mama sleep tonight," I tell him, careful to keep my voice quiet. "She finally married me today, you know. She's so stubborn. I think you get that from her. I waited a long time for her, and we waited a long time for you and your sister. I think that we were always supposed to be a family, the timing just wasn't right yet. But here you are, and I just couldn't love you any more than I do."

I kiss his forehead, and he yawns, so I place him on my shoulder and rub his back the way he likes.

"You should go back to sleep."

My own eyelids are heavy from lack of sleep. I really don't know what we would have done over the past two months without our family's help and our awesome friends. The first two weeks were overwhelming and scary, but we've figured out an eating and sleeping routine, and I think we're going to hire a nanny soon.

Mia is a wonderful mother. She knows that although the babies are her world, she also loves to cook. That's another important part of her life, and she wants to go back to the restaurant part time to start. I think it's imperative that she does what feeds her soul.

Ethan is softly snoring in my ear now, and I lay him back in his crib and pause, making sure he doesn't wake back up. When it seems safe, I tiptoe out of the nursery and next door to our bedroom, where Mia's sitting up in bed.

"I thought you were sleeping," I say and slide in next to her, pulling her into my arms. "Are you okay?"

"I'm great," she says. "I woke up too, and I was just listening in case Lizzy decided to join your little party."

"She's sleeping like a champ," I reply. "How do you feel?"

"Hmm," she says and slides her naked leg up along mine. "The babies are asleep, and we're awake."

"This is true."

Her hand glides down my chest and over my stomach, then wraps around my very hard cock.

"I thought I was too tired for this," I murmur and push her onto her back. "But you're so fucking beautiful in the moonlight."

"I'm sorry we don't do this enough," she says, but I press my fingertip over her lips.

"We'll get back to that place," I assure her. "We're figuring all of this out. And that's okay. I'm going to enjoy you every moment that I can, and that doesn't always have to include sex."

"But it's so nice when it does," she says with a smile, and tips her head back when I slide my hand down her belly to her core. She's already wet and ready for me, but I want to take my time.

I kiss down her torso, spending extra time licking and sucking on each nipple. Her breasts are slightly bigger than before, fitting perfectly into my palms. I worry her nipples with my thumbs as I kiss down her belly, around her navel, and farther still.

Her clit is hard against my lips.

"Bite it," she whispers, making me grin.

She's such a biter.

I oblige her, scraping my teeth over it, then gently biting it. She makes a strangled noise, trying to be quiet, and I climb up to cover her mouth with mine. I pin her hands above her head and she cradles me against her, urging me to grind my dick against her core.

Finally, unable to hold back any longer, I rear back and press the head of my cock inside of her and sink slowly down until I'm buried balls deep.

"So good," I whisper against her wet lips. "Always so fucking good."

I rock against her, rubbing my pubis against her clit and she gasps, bears down, and comes hard, her pussy contracting around me. She's got a fucking vise grip on me, and I can't stop myself from following her over the edge.

Once I've caught my breath, I pull her against me and kiss her forehead.

"You are the best part of this life, Mia."

"It's a good life," she agrees with a yawn. "It's a very good life."

Epilogue

Five years later . . .

~Mia~

I hate that we only do our Sunday brunches once a month now," Kat says with a frown and sips on her strawberry mimosa.

"At least we find time to do them at all," Cami reminds her. "I think this is the first time in more than seven years that none of us is pregnant, therefore making it possible for all of us to drink."

"Are we done having babies?" I ask, looking at Kat, who just had a brand-new baby boy two months ago. "Do you and Mac want more?"

"No," she says, shaking her fiery red head. "I could give

you all kinds of statistics about how many children you should have, and it would be incredibly boring. Let's just say that I'm happy with the one."

"I'm done," I reply with a nod. "Three is plenty. I didn't think I'd have more after the twins, who I'm convinced are evil, by the way. But then we got another surprise, and had Emily."

"I hope you all did something to prevent more surprise babies," Cami says.

"He did," I reply with a wink. "No need to worry anymore."

"Five's my limit," Addie says with a grin.

"You're a baby machine," Riley says. "And before you ask, no. Trevor and I are holding at two. One of each, that's perfect for us."

"We are lucky to have the one we do have," Cami says with a wistful smile. "We may think about adoption later; but for now, Landon and I are happy with it just being the three of us. Why are the twins evil?"

"They speak in tongues," I reply as I butter a piece of toast. "That can't be normal."

"I've heard that some twins make up their own language," Kat says. "That's fascinating."

"They stare at me while they speak to each other in a language I don't understand."

"Okay, that's creepy," Addie says. "But they're so damn cute."

"And they have us all wrapped around their little fingers," I agree. "If we could get them to start speaking English, we'd be golden."

"What does Camden think?"

"He laughs it off. Camden is so laid back, very little riles him up. Which is good because he's married to *me*, and I'm not exactly the definition of laid back."

"True," Addie says, earning a glare from me. She smiles angelically. "How did things go in New York last week?"

"Actually, not horrible." In the past few years, we've expanded the Seduction restaurants all over the United States, with Europe on the horizon. There are currently eight locations, with the most recent being New York. "The location is amazing, right down in Times Square. The chefs are great, of course. I mean, we're a successful, nichey restaurant. Who doesn't want to work for us?"

"That one guy in London wasn't excited about it," Addie reminds me, but I blow that off.

"His loss. We'll find someone else for London."

"I can't even believe we're expanding to Europe," Cami says, shaking her head. "Remember where we started? We wanted our *one* tiny location in Portland to *not* bankrupt us."

"And now here we are, seven years later, with a billion-dollar business." Riley raises her glass in a toast. "We're pretty fucking amazing, ladies."

"Hear, hear," I reply and clink my glass to hers.

"But at the end of the day," Kat reminds us, "not only do we have a successful business, but we've managed to stay friends too. And that's rare, you guys. I love you. Each of you. That's more important that the restaurants, the money, any of it."

"Of course," I add as the others nod. "As long as we have each other, there's not anything we can't do."

"Including Europe," Addie says with a grin. "They won't know what hit them."

Menu

Mia's Famous Apple Pie
Anne Vin Glacé, Anne Amie Vineyards,
Willamette Valley, Oregon, 2014

Camden's Award-Winning Cheesecake
Amie Vin Doux Naturel, Anne Amie Vineyards,
Willamette Valley, Oregon, 2014

Mia's Famous Apple Pie

Pie Dough:

15 oz. pastry flour
1 T. sugar
1 t. salt
½ cup shortening, cold
½ cup butter, cold
1 t. white vinegar
6 T. water, ice cold

1. Sift pastry flour and sugar together in medium bowl. Add salt and whisk together.
2. Cut in uniform pieces of shortening and cold butter.
3. Drizzle in white vinegar and then water to achieve soft dough. Note, if the dough is too dry, it will not roll out without excessive cracking. Make sure to use full amount of water.
4. Divide dough into two equal portions. Wrap tightly in plastic. Refrigerate until ready to roll out.

Apple Filling:
6 large Granny Smith apples
½ lemon
¼ cup white sugar
½ t. cinnamon

1. Peel and cut apples into ¼-inch-thick slices.
2. Toss apples with juice of ½ lemon, white sugar, and cinnamon.
3. Let sit for 15–30 minutes. Drain and pat dry, making sure to remove all excess moisture.

Syrup for Apples:
½ cup butter
3 T. all-purpose flour
2 t. water
½ cup white sugar
½ cup brown sugar
½ t. cinnamon
⅛ t. nutmeg
Pinch of clove

1. Melt butter in medium pan on stovetop, add flour, and stir, making sure that all flour has dissolved.
2. Add water, sugars, and spices and bring to a boil.
3. Cook for 2–3 minutes over medium heat until syrup has slightly thickened and bubbles are visible over the top of the syrup.

4. Pour over drained and dried apples, mix, and let cool to room temperature.

Crumble Topping:

1 cup flour
⅓ cup brown sugar
1½ t. cinnamon
1 t. salt
½ cup (1 stick) butter, cold

1. Add flour, brown sugar, cinnamon, and salt to a bowl. Cut in cold butter until mixture is cohesive but still crumbly. Set aside.

To assemble and bake pie:

1. Roll out one half of the saved pie dough and place into an 8-inch pie tin. Cut off excess dough.
2. Layer cooled apple slices in the pan so that there is little space between the apples and then pour leftover syrup into the pie over the tops of the apples.
3. Roll out second half of the pie dough. Using an egg wash, coat the edges of the pie dough (glue) and then place rolled-out dough on top of the pie, pressing lightly on the edges to adhere the two pieces. Cut off excess dough. Using the tines of a fork, make an impression to tightly seal the edges around the circumference of the pie.
4. Using a very sharp paring knife, cut a 4–5-inch diam-

eter circle on top of the crust, remove circle, and discard. Place the crumble on top of the pie, making sure to cover the exposed apples.

5. Brush egg wash on top of the pie crust only. Bake on the bottom rack of the oven at 375°F for 30 minutes. Turn down the oven to 350°F and bake for an additional 20–30 minutes until the crust and crumble are golden brown.

Camden's Award-Winning Cheesecake

Crust:
1½ cups graham cracker crumbs
⅓ cup white sugar
⅔ cup melted butter

1. Place graham cracker crumbs and white sugar in a bowl and mix together. Add melted butter and mix until all butter has been incorporated.
2. Press into bottom of 9-inch springform pan. Bake at 350°F for 10 minutes until golden brown. Set aside to cool while making filling.

Cheesecake Filling:
2 lbs. cream cheese, room temperature
1¾ cup white sugar
2½ T. cornstarch
6 eggs
1½ t. vanilla extract
8 oz. plain or vanilla yogurt

1. In a mixer with a paddle attachment, mix cream cheese, sugar, and cornstarch until smooth, about 2–3 minutes on medium speed. Scrape down bowl.
2. On slow speed, add eggs one at a time, making sure each is fully incorporated before adding the next egg. Continue until all eggs are incorporated. Add vanilla extract. Scrape down bowl.
3. Add yogurt in two parts on medium speed until fully combined. Your batter should be creamy and smooth and free of lumps. Scrape down bowl. If there are a few lumps, mix on medium speed for 30 seconds—do not overmix at this stage.
4. Pour cream cheese batter into pan over crust. Do not overfill. Bake at 325°F for 45–60 minutes. Check cheesecake by inserting a sharp knife in the center. If it comes out clean and there is no jiggle to the cake, it is done. If the cake is not done, bake in 5-minute increments until knife inserted in center comes out clean.
5. Remove from oven and let cool to room temperature. Refrigerate up to 4 hours or overnight before serving. Top with fresh strawberries or raspberry sauce or chocolate sauce.

Jake's song for Addie, "If I Had Never Met You," specially written and recorded for *Listen to Me*, is available for purchase from music retailers!

Kristenprobyauthor.com/listentomesong

Up next from *New York Times* bestselling author
Kristen Proby, the Romancing Manhattan series
follows three brothers who get more than they
bargain for as they navigate love in New York
City! The first romance in this new series,

ALL THE WAY

On Sale Summer 2018!

BOOKS BY KRISTEN PROBY

LISTEN TO ME
A Fusion Novel; Book One

Seduction is quickly becoming the hottest new restaurant in Portland, a Addison Wade is proud to claim her share of the credit. But when forr rock star Jake Keller swaggers through the doors to apply for the weeke gig, she knows she's in trouble. He's all bad boy . . . exactly her type a exactly what she doesn't need.

CLOSE TO YOU
A Fusion Novel; Book Two

Since the day she met Landon Palazzo, Camilla LaRue, part owner of the wildly popular restaurant Seduction, has been head-over-heels in love. And when Landon joined the Navy right after high school, Cami thought her heart would never recover. But it did, and all these years later, she's managed to not only survive, but thrive. But now, Landon is back and he looks better than ever.

BLUSH FOR ME
A Fusion Novel; Book Three

When Kat, the fearless, no-nonsense bar manager of Seduction, and Mac successful but stubborn business owner, find themselves unable to play n or even keep their hands off each other, it'll take some fine wine and ev hotter chemistry for them to admit they just might be falling in love.

THE BEAUTY OF US
A Fusion Novel; Book Four

Riley Gibson is over the moon at the prospect of having her restaurant, Seduction, on the Best Bites TV network. This could be the big break she's been waiting for. But the idea of having an in-house show on a regular basis is a whole other matter. Riley knows it's an opportunity she can't afford to pass on. And when she meets Trevor Cooper, the show's executive producer, she's stunned by their intense chemistry.

SAVOR YOU
A Fusion Novel; Book Five

Cooking isn't what Mia Palazzo does, it's who she is. Food is her passion... pride...her true love. She's built a stellar menu for her restaurant, Seduct Now, after being open for only a few short years, Mia's restaurant is be featured on Best Bites TV. Then Camden Sawyer, the biggest mistake of life, walks into her kitchen... As Mia and Camden face off, neither realizes high the stakes are as their reputations are put on the line and their hearts put to the ultimate test.